LOVE OR TITLE

THE COLCHESTER SISTERS

CHARLOTTE DARCY

FAIR HAVENS BOOKS

SWEET REGENCY ROMANCE

Charlotte Darcy writes sweet Regency romance that will take you back to a time when life was a little more magical.

Fall in love again,

Charlotte Darcy

*E*sme Colchester sat at her dressing table contentedly listening to the chatter of her younger sisters. All three of the young Colchester women were looking forward to the garden party at the home of Lord and Lady Hollerton but for entirely different reasons.

Whilst Jane Colchester hoped for romance and Verity Colchester hoped to see Mrs. Peron to secure an invite to an evening botany lecture, Esme's wants were a little more serious.

At nearly one-and-twenty, Esme was looking for a husband, and not just any man would do. Esme Colchester had done her reading and knew every little thing a man ought to have in order to be considered a good prospect.

"You look a little serious, Esme," Jane said as she and their maid tried to weave dried flowers through a struggling Verity's hair. "Oh Verity! Do sit still."

"I am not at all serious," Esme replied reassuringly. "I am very much looking forward to the day. I do so love a garden party, especially when the summer is just beginning."

"As do I," Jane continued. "But I still think you look a little serious; after all, parties of any kind are for fun."

"I suppose my thoughts drift to my prospects now and again," Esme said with a sigh. "Or lack thereof."

"How on earth does a beautiful young woman of good breeding lack prospects?" Jane asked incredulously. "There is many a young man in the world who would trip over his own feet to get to you. The problem is, you will not allow them an opportunity. You do not get to know them."

"What is the point when they are not suitable?" Esme said a little defensively.

Her sister, Jane, was a hopeless romantic who would gladly see Esme married to an impoverished poet as long as she loved him.

"Oh, here we go," Verity said with an amused laugh in an aside to the maid, Violet, who smiled but wisely remained silent.

Esme sighed; Jane would never understand her need for such stability when the truth was that she hardly understood it herself. But the fact was that Esme had a very determined view of what a good match looked like, and she had yet to find that most elusive thing for herself.

"Oh, Esme, I do wish you would give this up. There are many fine young men out there, they do not need to have everything on your list of wants," Jane said gently. "What is title and privilege against the more important things; character, kindness, and mostly, love?"

"But I am the eldest daughter, Jane. I really must make a good marriage to give you and Verity the very best advantages. Where one good marriage falls within a family, others are bound to follow. It sets a precedent and it tells society at large that the

Colchester family are still very fine. They are still worth marrying."

"Of course, we *are* a very fine family, my dear. And as for myself and Verity, you need not worry. Truly, I would much rather see you marry for love than marry for our prospects. You agree with me, do you not, Verity?" Jane asked and took the opportunity to thread another flower through her younger sister's hair whilst she was suitably diverted by the question.

"I wish you would not even think of such things, Esme. I for one want *never* to marry, it would not suit me at all. And so, you see, you would do me no favors by marrying a man just because he is everything that society finds acceptable. As far as I can see, he need only be acceptable to you." Verity, just seventeen-years-old, was extraordinarily intelligent. "Enough flowers, Jane. There will be more flowers in my hair than in Lord and Lady Hollerton's garden."

"It is not just for the sake of my sisters, I must admit. There are so many considerations when choosing a husband. And I should so like to find a man who has everything that I have always wished for. Is it really so wrong to want such things? To aspire to a good marriage, even a little title, such fine prospects for my children when I have them?" Esme smiled at her sisters, wondering how it was that three young women brought up so close together could be so very different.

Jane shook her head. "Of course, it is not wrong to want those things. Forgive me, my dear, I should never have made you feel that it was. You know how I am, you know I am a romantic. I am just worried that you would marry a man for all the things that society sees as good instead of questioning your own heart for your own standards of goodness." Jane gave up with Verity's hair and dropped the last of the flowers into her sister's lap before scowling at her. "You really are a dreadful fidget!"

"And you are terribly bossy," Verity complained. "I did not want flowers in my hair, you did!"

"If I do not marry soon, I will be forced to listen to the pair of you arguing until I am an old maid." Esme laughed, enjoying the camaraderie which had always existed between them.

Despite there being three, they never split or formed alliances of two. They were as close as it was possible for sisters to be, whatever their differences, and Esme knew that she would miss them dreadfully when the time really did come for her to marry.

"Is there really such a hurry for you to marry?" Verity said sensibly. "Not to escape your sisters, you understand." She laughed. "I suppose I do not understand the urgency."

"My age, for one thing," Esme said.

"But you are still only twenty." Verity shrugged.

"There are many young ladies married by my age."

"Yes, but when you have time and exceedingly good parents, you have the opportunity to make a good choice. Papa has never put any pressure on any of us to make the sort of marriage that you are hoping for. But my dear, you speak as if you will be an old maid and living here forever. If anyone is going to do that, it is going to be me. And by choice, I might add," Verity said vehemently. "Dear Amos, he said that I might stay here with him forever when he finally inherits Papa's estate."

"It is true, we are very fortunate in terms of both our parents and our brother. Dear Amos, he would keep all three of us here forever given the opportunity."

Esme smiled. "I wonder if he ever feels left out having three sisters," she mused, changing the subject for a moment to give herself some respite.

"I think he considers himself to have the best of both worlds." Jane laughed. "He can be in our company if he wants and claim us to be silly females and make himself scarce without causing too much offense when he wants to be rid of us. But he is a dear, Verity, just as you say."

"But to get back to the original topic of conversation," Verity said in a most determined manner. "I think you should be very careful not to rush into anything, Esme. You are very beautiful and very clever, and you need not settle upon any man who is not suitable, even if he is titled and will raise our status a little. For having a title or great wealth does not necessarily ensure that sense, intelligence, or any type of interesting character-filled personality at all comes along with it."

"In the end I suppose it is all a moot point." Esme was beginning to wish that the conversation had never begun. "After all, what man of title is going to have a moment's interest in me?"

"What man of sense would *not* have an interest in you?" Jane stated with determination.

"What sisters we are!" Esme laughed. "I wish to make a sensible marriage, Jane wishes to make a romantic one, and Verity wishes to avoid the whole subject altogether."

"At least it is never dull when we three are together," Verity said. "Now, I suppose we ought to make our way down to the carriage before our parents simply leave without us."

"Yes, we must go." Esme rose from her seat at the dressing table and ducked her head to hide the worry that crossed her face. Would she ever find a suitable prospect?

CHAPTER 2

*L*ord and Lady Hollerton lived in a very fine and large country mansion in Hertfordshire, just a twenty-minute carriage ride from the Colchester's estate.

Lord Hollerton, a Baron, was a nice man, one Esme had always liked. He was a little older than her father and always spoke to the Colchester girls as if they were his own daughters. He was, despite being aged, the epitome of a fine society aristocrat. If only she could make her sisters see that it was the roundedness of such men as Lord Hollerton which had helped her to form her own ideas of a fine husband.

Lord Hollerton was a man of title and wealth and his

children had been raised with every advantage. And yet, at the same time, they had been raised with humility and were all very fine and well respected, not to mention well-liked. Why could Esme not want the same for herself as Lady Hollerton had found?

As far as Esme was aware, Lady Hollerton had come from the upper echelons of the vast middle class, having been born into circumstances much like her own. The Colchester estate was large and long-lived, having been in the family for generations, was upper middle class, and enjoyed a decent wealth.

The Colchesters were invited just about everywhere, being popular and well-respected. Surely, there was no reason that she could not be as successful as dear Lady Hollerton in the marriage arena?

"Oh, smell the wonderful scented stocks. How clever to have them all around the edges of the lawn." Verity, a lover of nature, was effusive. "I could stand with my eyes closed breathing this in forever."

"I think the Hollertons would have some little objection to that in the end." Elizabeth Colchester, their mother, was a wonderful woman.

Her children meant the world to her and the

relationship she had with her daughters was precious. She was a woman of quick wit, much like Verity, and she had a great propensity to gentle teasing.

"I suppose they would." Verity laughed prettily and took her father's arm. "It is a beautiful garden for such a party though, is it not?"

"Very beautiful." Mrs. Colchester agreed. "It reminds me that I ought to take a little more interest in our own."

"Oh dear," Esme said humorously. "Remember poor Mr. Perkins' expression the last time you interfered in the garden, Mama?"

"He is very territorial. But I ought to stand up to him once in a while." Mrs. Colchester began to laugh before squinting off into the distance.

"What is it, Mama?" Esme asked as she took her mother's arm.

"A man staring," Mrs. Colchester said under her breath. "But no matter, he has looked away now."

"We must not tell Papa that a man was staring at you," Esme said teasingly.

She looked ahead of her to where her father was standing. Both Verity and Jane had joined him, leaving Esme and her mother trailing behind.

"It was not me he stared at, my dear. His gaze was fixed upon you. So fixed, I might add, that he did not realize immediately that I had seen him." Mrs. Colchester's tone was both protective and disapproving.

"Oh? Which man?" Esme asked, suddenly keen to see him.

"Esme, do not look over there," Mrs. Colchester said, drawing her daughter's attention. "But if you must see him, he is the man wearing a blue tailcoat with cream breeches. He is very tall and has fair hair."

"Right," Esme said and tried to look nonchalant as she let her eyes sweep back in his direction.

She saw him immediately, and he saw her. Her performance of idly looking about her without intent had fallen flat on its face.

Esme, having only a vague impression of the man, tall, fair, and well-dressed, looked hurriedly away.

"Oh, do let us move along," she said, feeling embarrassed that he had seen her searching for him.

"Indeed." Her mother turned. "Oh, here comes Lady Longton," Mrs. Colchester said warmly. "I met her at a charity event last week."

"Lady Longton?" Esme said, her interest piqued. "Is she not the mother of the Marquis of Longton?"

"She is." Mrs. Colchester shrugged as if it was nothing. "Good afternoon, Lady Longton," she said as the woman finally joined them.

"Mrs. Colchester, how nice to see you again. What a pleasing result from the charity drive last week." Lady Longton seemed like a very nice woman as far as Esme could tell.

There was a warmth about her, an air of approachability, much like that displayed by Lord and Lady Hollerton.

Proof, if more were needed, that people with titles were as pleasant as anybody else. She would remember to tell Jane all about it for it might go some way to soothing that romantic heart of hers.

"We raised such a lot of money for good causes, Lady

Longton. It is gratifying to have been so successful," Mrs. Colchester went on. "I do not believe you have met my eldest daughter." She turned to smile at Esme with ease and warmth. "This is Esme. And Esme, this is Lady Longton."

"I am very pleased to meet you, Lady Longton," Esme said and inclined her head gracefully.

Esme had practiced such things until she ached and knew that she could be introduced to any member of society and behave well.

"How wonderful to meet you at last. Your mother speaks well of you." She smiled and seemed genuinely pleased to meet Esme. "But then we mothers tend to do that."

"Indeed." Mrs. Colchester laughed.

"And here comes my own child," Lady Longton said as a painfully handsome young man began to make his way to them. "Although he does not allow me to call him that. He is a grown man, even if he will always be my little boy."

Esme was torn between a deep sense of warmth for dear Lady Longton, and tongue-tying excitement at the prospect of meeting such a perfect-looking man.

The Marquis was truly handsome. He had the darkest hair and the bluest eyes she had ever seen. And his hair was thick and unruly, making him look pleasingly roguish.

"My dear, how nice." Lady Longton looked thrilled that her son was to join them. "I must introduce you to Mrs. Colchester and her lovely daughter, Esme."

"Mrs. Colchester," he said with a handsome smiled and a gracious bow.

"This is my son, Daniel Winsford, the Marquis of Longton." Lady Longton introduced her son with such pride that Esme found herself all the more nervous.

"What a pleasure to meet you, My Lord," Mrs. Colchester, despite the formality of her greeting, was still a picture of ease and poise; Esme hoped that she could find a little of that poise for herself.

"And Miss Colchester, I am charmed to make your acquaintance," he said and looked into her eyes before bowing again.

"I am pleased to meet you, Lord Longton," Esme said and felt her cheeks brighten with sudden shyness.

"Tell me, do you know my mother through her charitable works?" he asked, aiming the question at both mother and daughter.

"Indeed, Lady Longton and I are recent acquaintances, having met at Lady Denton's charity drive." Mrs. Colchester smiled.

"And I have only just made Miss Colchester's acquaintance, Daniel." Lady Longton gave Esme a smile of encouragement. "Oh, what a nice afternoon this promises to be."

"Indeed, it does," the Marquis said and looked directly at Esme.

CHAPTER 3

"Oh, my goodness!" Elizabeth Colchester burst into the drawing room in a way which made the occupants jump. "Forgive me." She went on apologetically. "But we have an invitation from the Marquis of Longton."

"Oh yes?" Edward Colchester said with a vague sort of enthusiasm. "What is the event, my dear?" He smiled benignly at his wife.

"Afternoon tea. The invitation is for me, you, and Esme. And it is for Wednesday afternoon." Still standing, Mrs. Colchester waved the thick invitation card this way and that.

"Oh, what on earth am I going to wear?" Esme asked,

nerves and excitement swirling around the walls of her chest.

"This is exciting," Jane said in a breathy manner. "He is very handsome. And he seemed attentive at the garden party, even though Papa would not let the rest of us join you." She gave her father a mock disappointed look which he seemed to enjoy thoroughly.

Although Daniel and his mother had spent no more than twenty minutes with Esme and her mother, she had been pleased that her father had kept Jane and Verity back. Not that they would have done anything at all to upset things, for she was always pleased to be with her sisters in public. But he had likely seen how fragile she had felt to be introduced to such a fine young man and how further introductions and awkward conversations might have done something to disrupt it.

As much as he claimed not to understand the feminine world, Edward Colchester seemed to have a natural instinct for such things.

"Well, I thought it would be all too complicated if the three of us joined them," Mr. Colchester said with an amused smile. "What with you looking for any signs of true love in his eyes and Verity trying to frighten him away." He chuckled and was visibly pleased when his family joined in.

"Oh, Papa!" Esme said, feeling the flush of being the center of things. "You do tease."

"It is one of life's few pleasures."

"Is that so?" Elizabeth Colchester forgot all about the invitation for a moment as she placed her hands on her hips and tried not to laugh as she scowled at her husband.

"*One of.*" Edward looked sheepish.

"Was the Marquis a nice man, Esme?" Verity asked in a more serious tone than the rest of her family.

"Yes, very nice indeed," Esme said, remembering his dark hair and blue eyes and smiling at the thought.

"He was a polite young man," her mother agreed. "But really, a person would need more than twenty minutes to decide upon his character."

"You did not like him, Mama?" Esme asked a little defensively.

"What I saw of him I liked, my dear. But we are going to afternoon tea at Longton Hall, so I am certain we will find out a little more of his character then. These are early days, are they not?"

"Early days?" Esme felt a little flat suddenly.

Her mother had come into the drawing room with such excitement and now it seemed as if the whole thing was going to be ruined by misplaced common sense. For Esme was certain that she was a good judge of character and even more certain that she could have the measure of a person in no time at all. As far as she could see, Daniel Winsford had everything a young man should in terms of status *and* character. Oh, and he was really very handsome. So handsome that she had hardly slept for thinking about him ever since the garden party.

"I know how you are when it comes to choosing a young man, Esme. I would not want you to be blinded by everything that he is before you truly know him. I suppose I am advising you not to become fixed upon him. After all, there are a lot of nice young men out in the world." Her mother spoke in the soothing tones which had always marked Esme's childhood out as warm and wonderful.

"As you say, I will be able to get to know him better when we go to Longton Hall," Esme said, not wanting to argue with the mother she loved so dearly.

"He seemed very interested in you, Esme," Jane said, and it was clear she was determined to be excited about it all.

"How do you know? Have you not just complained that I kept you out of the way?" Their father was amusing himself again.

"I could tell by the way he stood," Jane said defiantly, and all present laughed. "You might find it amusing, but it is true. He turned towards you and looked directly at you whenever you spoke. Really, I thought he was quite charming."

"He *was* charming," Esme said gratefully.

"But he could have been saying anything, Jane." Edward Colchester was not ready to let it go.

"Papa!" Jane said. "Really! You are not helping at all."

"Then I shall keep quiet and promise faithfully to behave myself at Longton Hall." He stared off into the middle distance, his greying hair and pale blue eyes full of amusement. He was a much-adored father. "Imagine it, Mr. and Mrs. Colchester being invited to the home of a Marquis. How on earth is a simple man like me to afford such a dowry?"

"Papa! It is only afternoon tea!" Esme said, and the room became raucous again.

"What on earth is going on?" Amos, the eldest of the Colchester offspring, came into the drawing room wide-eyed and ready to join in.

He had been out riding and looked healthy and fresh, smelling a little of the outdoors, like dried linen brought in from the washing line.

"Esme has finally found a young man who fits her ideas of suitability, nay *society's* ideas, and he has invited her to tea with Mama and Papa on Wednesday," Verity said, reducing the whole thing to its most basic parts.

"Thank you, Verity, for your brevity," Amos said as he wandered into the room, pausing to ruffle Verity's already ruffled hair en route. "Nobody tells a tale like you do, my dear."

"What do you think of it all?" Jane asked, making room on the pretty but uncomfortable brocade-covered couch for her brother to sit beside her. "Esme met him at Lord and Lady Hollerton's garden party."

"I am sorry I missed it now," Amos said and laughed. "But who are we talking about? Who is this fine young man who meets every one of Esme's stringent requirements?" In temperament and humor, Amos Colchester was much like his father.

"Daniel Winsford," Esme said shyly. "He is the Mar..." She began, but Amos cut in.

"The Marquis of Longton," he said with confidence.

"Oh, do you know him?" Esme asked excitedly.

"I know of him and I have seen him from time to time at hunting events." He shrugged. "You found him pleasing?" Amos seemed tentative.

"Yes, his manners were very nice indeed." Esme was wondering if she was imagining Amos' change in demeanor.

"And you are to go to Longton Hall on Wednesday?" he went on.

"Yes, we are to go to afternoon tea."

"I believe that Lady Longton is a most pleasant lady," Amos said with enthusiasm.

"Oh yes, she is." Their mother came back into the conversation, keen to sing the praises of the Marquis' mother.

And, as the family began to discuss Lady Longton and her mother's connection to that fine woman, Esme studied her brother for any sign that he knew more of the Marquis than he had said. But for all the world, Esme could see nothing out of the ordinary.

CHAPTER 4

*L*ongton Hall appeared quite suddenly after what seemed like the longest estate driveway she had ever been on. But of course, it *was* the longest driveway she had ever seen because it was the largest estate she had ever been to.

Although the Colchesters had been invited to many fine events and were a well-respected family of some considerable wealth, invitations to the homes of Barons formed the larger part of their society experience. Earls, Marquises, and Dukes were quite something else altogether.

And Longton Hall, when she first looked upon it, was enough to take Esme Colchester's breath away. It was built in immaculate grey stone with the warm sunshine reflected in dozens of windows on the front elevation alone.

When their carriage drew up on the graveled front of Longton Hall, Esme could see that the wide stone steps leading to an immaculate flag stoned platform outside the immense doors were easily as large as the drawing room of her father's fine manor house.

Two footmen stood one on either side of the doorway in their fine livery, their responsibility nothing more than standing sentinel as their master's guests made their way inside.

The butler, austere but still managing to be welcoming, smiled at them and she was sure that he could sense a little of the family's nervousness on their first visit to such a fine and imposing home.

"Mr. Colchester, Mrs. Colchester." The butler nodded as he bowed. "And Miss Colchester." He reserved a small smile for the youngest in the party of three. "His Lordship and Lady Longton are awaiting you in the drawing room, if you would care to follow me."

"Thank you," Edward Colchester said in a firm and easy tone which made Esme proud of him.

Esme and her parents followed the butler, pausing in the great entrance hall to remove their light summer outerwear and the ladies' bonnets before proceeding.

By the time they reached the door to the sitting room, Esme was already a dreadful bundle of nerves. And not only was she nervous, but she was also lost.

They had taken so many turns through so many corridors and passed so many heavy oak doors that she was certain she would never find her way out of the building alone. Not, of course, that she imagined she would need to, but it crossed her mind nonetheless.

Esme looked down at herself appraisingly, hoping at this late stage that she had put enough effort in. She had been keen to dress well for the afternoon, but equally keen not to overdo things and show herself up as being inexperienced in such situations.

Her parents had not worried at all, although it was clear that they were dressed appropriately. But perhaps that was simply a facet of being older and settled in life, such worries did not concern one as they once did.

But Esme had chosen very carefully, making sure, as

always, that she wore a color most suitable to her chestnut hair which always seemed just a little redder in the summertime. She had picked a muted pale green gown in a heavy cotton. It had a dark green wide satin band beneath the bust and its sleeves were short and puffed with a little lace trim around the cuff.

The fabric itself was embroidered with a thread of the same color as the gown. The small embroidery flowers were neat and discreet but gave the fabric of her gown a wonderful depth.

Her maid, Violet, had helped to curl her hair into beautiful shining chestnut ringlets, with just one or two of the shorter ringlets falling in front of her ears and framing her face expertly. The rest of her thick hair had been neatly pinned up and Esme had been very pleased with the result.

"Good afternoon, Mr. Colchester and Mrs. Colchester." The Marquis was the first to his feet, bowing neatly at his guests. "And Miss Colchester." He bowed a little deeper to Esme and smiled at her.

But there was something in his smile which seemed a little different somehow. He did not strike Esme as being quite as much at ease as he had been at Lord and Lady Hollerton's garden party. But of course, he was the one doing the entertaining now, and Esme knew herself that it could sometimes be a little fraught.

"Good afternoon, Lord Longton." Esme smiled at him sweetly and inclined her head.

"Well, do come in, my dears," Lady Longton said, appearing at her son's side and fussing in the warm and wonderful way of a mother hen.

Esme had to admit to herself secretly that she was glad of Lady Longton and her kindly ways in that moment. Something about that lady certainly put her at her ease and she gave silent thanks for her.

No sooner were they all seated than the household servants began to make their way in with the most sumptuous afternoon tea Esme had ever set eyes on. There was bread-and-butter, cakes of all shapes and colors with cream on the top, fruits and sweets made out of sugar, all manner of wonderful things.

It looked so good, in fact, that Esme wished she did not feel quite so nervous for she would have liked to not only eat it but enjoy it too. Of course, a young lady ought never to overdo things, but perhaps she would have enjoyed a little cake.

"I must say, I did enjoy Lord and Lady Hollerton's garden party," Lady Longton said, beginning a little conversation amongst them all as soon as the afternoon tea had been served.

"Yes, it was a very pleasant afternoon. The weather was perfect." As her mother spoke, Esme wished she had a little of her confidence.

"And you enjoyed it greatly did you not, Daniel?" Lady Longton looked to her son.

Esme, who had sat shyly fixated upon the ornate teapot, allowed her eyes to wander to where Daniel Winsford sat. He was in an armchair not quite opposite where Esme sat on a large and comfortable couch with her mother.

He looked as handsome as he had done the first time she had set eyes on him. His dark hair was wonderfully thick and unruly and his blue eyes so blue that she wished she had the confidence to look into them for a moment. He was wearing black breeches and knee boots with a waistcoat and tailcoat in a shade of green not dissimilar to the gown she was wearing. Esme smiled to herself, imagining that her sister Jane would think their unwitting choice of such similar colors meant something romantic.

"Immensely," the Marquis answered his mother with a single word.

Esme studied him a little more closely, taken aback at the shortness of his answer and what little of his tone she had gleaned from that single word. But it was his look more than anything else; the way he had momentarily surveyed his mother with annoyance.

Esme wondered if the two of them had argued, or at least had some cross words, before she and her parents had arrived.

"I am bound to say that Lord Hollerton's gardener certainly knows his business," Esme's father added to the conversation with ease and grace and she knew in her heart that he sought to spare Lady Longton any little embarrassment her son's seeming disinterest might have caused her. "Tell me, Lady Longton, did you manage to visit the little camellia garden? It really was quite something."

"I did, Mr. Colchester," Lady Longton said with

enthusiasm and, Esme thought, a little relief. "Such shades of pink as I have never seen. What a wonderful display. I have rarely been as impressed by camellias as I was at Hollerton Hall."

"The grounds here at Longton Hall are very fine," Esme's mother added.

"Thank you kindly, Mrs. Colchester. Perhaps when we have finished our tea you might care to see the gardens at the back of the hall. The head gardener here is a very attentive man. He has been here at Longton since he was a boy."

"Oh yes, I should like that very much," Mrs. Colchester said and turned a little in her seat to look at her daughter, quietly indicating that she ought to speak.

"Yes, it is such a fine day to be outside," Esme added, surprised that she recognized her voice as rather normal.

Her insides felt absolutely rigid and she could hardly believe that it did not show in her tone of voice. But perhaps, given the opportunity to get to know the Marquis better, she might not feel quite so nervous and out of place.

The afternoon tea went on in much the same vein, with the parents in the party very much holding up the conversation on their own shoulders. The Marquis sat in his armchair so rigidly and with such a look of unapproachability that it rendered Esme mute also.

Once or twice, Esme was certain that she had seen little flashes of exasperation on the lined and pleasant face of Lady Longton. And in truth, she could hardly blame her, for it seemed for all the world as if the Marquis was not at all pleased to be in their company.

If only he could talk and behave as he had done at the garden party, so lightly and warmly. If only he would look at her now as Jane claimed he had, his very manner full of interest for everything that she had to say.

And things were a little better when they made their way outside, although she was pleased to be released from the all too large drawing room. To be able to walk outside in the sunshine and have displays and lawns pointed out to her that she might easily and readily comment upon seemed to take the pressure off her somehow and Esme found her tongue once more.

"And these are my camellias, of course. Very beautiful, but I am bound to say not nearly as beautiful as the display of camellias that we saw at the garden party, Mr. Colchester." Lady Longton was ahead of the little group with Esme's mother and father, chattering happily as she went.

"Your grounds really are very beautiful, Lord Longton," Esme said, speaking quietly to the Marquis as if to be overheard would make her a little embarrassed.

The truth was, it had taken all her courage to utter those few words, all the while wondering if his response would be anywhere near favorable. If it were not, she had determined to say nothing else to him for the rest of the day.

"Thank you, Miss Colchester," he said, turning to look at her briefly as they walked.

He was a tall man with a pleasing shape and he walked along in easy strides with his hands gently clasped behind his back. "I must admit, I have very little to do with it all. Gardening and what have you has seldom interested me, and I am of a mind that the gardener is paid to be left to it." He smiled briefly, and Esme felt her heart leap; such small crumbs from him providing so much pleasure. "Although I do believe that my mother interferes regularly."

"As does mine with our gardener, Lord Longton. I think it is on every mother's list of things to do."

"Quite so," he said and laughed good-naturedly if not heartily.

At that point, Lady Longton took them all off in a different direction altogether, walking them down to the lake as she gave her commentary on every part of the grounds and gardens. It naturally put an end to the tentative conversation between the two young people and Esme felt a little relieved.

She wanted those last few minutes to be what she remembered of the day, the pleasant little conversation she had shared with the Marquis. In his current mood, she wondered if to continue the conversation would be to risk losing those few moments of magic, and that was something that she did not want to do.

And so, when they climbed up into the carriage at the end of the afternoon, Esme had already convinced herself that she had enjoyed the whole thing. There had been enough conversation between them to run over and over in her mind when she was back home and in the quiet of her own chamber.

She would remember his handsome face and his smile as they had talked of their mothers and she would focus upon it. And as for his curious mood for the rest of the afternoon, well, everybody had their bad days, did they not?

CHAPTER 5

*E*sme had chosen to wear a rich cream gown with a heavy lace overlay for the summer ball at the home of Lord Berkeley. Its only adornment was a pale green band beneath the bust and she wore it with long white gloves.

Her hair was in ringlets again, just as it had been when she went to afternoon tea at Longton Hall. But this time she had longer curls hanging down and grazing her shoulders instead of just shorter ones framing her face.

She had a pretty comb in the side of her hair with some dainty paper flowers on it, just large enough to be seen and small enough to be discreet. All in all,

Esme felt comfortable. She was pleased with her appearance.

The ballroom at Berkeley Hall was vast and had been decorated with great vases of summer flowers set on tall pedestals all about the place. Esme could detect their fragrance everywhere and breathed in deeply to enjoy it. She had a good feeling about the evening and she felt a knot of nervous pleasure in her stomach every time she thought about the Marquis. He was likely already here somewhere, all she had to do was find him.

Of course, she did not intend to make herself obvious. Instead she would stand a few feet away with her sisters, seemingly oblivious to his presence, and wait for the Marquis to make the first move.

With Mr. and Mrs. Colchester deep in conversation with Lord and Lady Hollerton, Esme and her sisters began to gently work their way through the ballroom.

"There he is." Verity was the first to spy him as he stood in the middle of a group of five or six people.

"Then let us stand here, for we are close enough," Esme said and stood sideways onto the group, her face determinedly turned towards her sisters.

"So now we just stand here in the hope that he notices you?" Verity said and seemed quietly annoyed with the whole thing.

But Verity was young and determined not to understand the way things were out in society and very likely thought that Esme could simply walk up to the man and bid him good evening.

"That is the idea, yes," Esme said with a hint of exasperation. "I cannot simply insert myself into his party, you see."

"I do not see why you have to search for him at all. If he likes you well enough, Esme, then surely he might search for you instead. It strikes me that you are not going to enjoy the ball standing here all night sideways onto him and aching from such impossibly perfect posture."

"If you are not at all happy to be with us this evening, Verity, you could always return to Mama and Papa and take part in the conversation with Lord and Lady Hollerton." Esme knew she was being waspish, but she was nervous enough without Verity's determined common sense.

There was no place for common sense at a society ball, surely.

"My dear, the Marquis has seen you and he is smiling," Jane said discreetly, doing her best to hide her excitement. "He has his head tilted to one side and has made eye contact with me, Esme. I think you must turn now to acknowledge him."

"Right, I shall do just that," Esme said and hesitated for a moment.

She felt suddenly far less nervous and rather more afraid than she had done before. She began to question herself, to wonder if she had played her cards of behavior and etiquette correctly. Perhaps she had not, perhaps she had been obvious and therefore lacking polish.

"Esme, you must acknowledge him," Jane said with a little hint of panic in her voice.

Esme immediately turned her head, her heart lurching when she looked into his face. She inclined her head gracefully and was so relieved when he smiled at her that she could have fainted. The wave of relief made her feel a little weak and she realized just how afraid she had been that he would not notice her or, if he did, that he would not pay her any heed whatsoever.

But that was all her mother's talk upsetting her, she was sure of it. Mrs. Colchester had been determined to make her daughter aware that she need never accept any invitations that she did not want to accept. It did not matter who they were from, she did not have to spend time in anybody's company if she did not find them agreeable.

Esme had known immediately that her mother was talking of the Marquis and she had found herself defending the man, telling her mother how perfectly pleasant he had been out in the grounds of Longton Hall. But her mother simply nodded and smiled sweetly, her mind clearly already made up about Daniel Winsford.

When the Marquis broke free from his little party for a moment and began to walk towards her, Esme's heart was beating like a drum. He stopped in front of her, his black breeches and tailcoat immaculate against his golden colored waistcoat and white shirt. His thick dark hair looked good enough for her to reach out and touch, although she knew she would never do such a thing.

"Miss Colchester, how lovely to see you here," he said in the tone of one who was surprised that she was there at all.

Her mother and his had discussed their attendance at the Berkeley ball when they had afternoon tea, but perhaps the Marquis had been a little out of sorts, or at least had not paid much attention.

"I hope you are well, My Lord," Esme said and inclined her head again, seemingly amusing him.

"Indeed, I am well," he said and was smiling. "Come, let me introduce you to my party." He held out his arm for her to take.

Esme caught Jane's eye and saw her sister nod that she should go, that she should leave her and Verity behind and not worry about it.

"Please allow me to introduce you to my cousin, Miss Colchester. This is Lady Rachel Marlow and she has come to stay at Longton Hall for a few weeks."

"I am pleased to meet you, My Lady," Esme said shyly.

"And I am pleased to meet you, Miss Colchester."

Lady Rachel smiled at her warmly, reminding Esme greatly of Lady Longton.

There was an ease and kindness about the woman that she immediately liked.

"And these are my friends, Miss Colchester," the Marquis went on in a tone she did not quite recognize. She felt a little embarrassment when she thought it might be amusement on his part. "This is Michael Burton and his sisters, Miss Eliza Burton and Miss Henrietta Burton."

"How nice to meet you, Miss Colchester." Michael Burton was ostentatiously dressed compared to the Marquis, but he was polite if not friendly as he performed a little bow.

"I am pleased to make your acquaintance, Mr. Burton." Esme turned to Mr. Burton's sisters only to find that they had already begun to speak amongst themselves again and had no intention of going through with the full and formal introduction.

Something about it made Esme feel small, parochial almost, as if her simple manners were somehow old-fashioned. But surely manners were never old-fashioned, and the sisters were behaving rather poorly.

"Miss Colchester's mother is a friend of my mother," the Marquis said as if to explain her presence. "Mrs. Colchester does charitable works as my mother does, and that is how they have come to be acquainted, is it not?" He narrowed his eyes and looked at Esme for confirmation.

"Yes, that is quite true," Esme said, feeling a little silly and wondering where this was all going to end.

"And my mother invited Miss Colchester and her parents for afternoon tea last week. So there, now our connection is explained," he said and barked a little laugh.

All three Burtons barked along with him, the sisters, Eliza and Henrietta, rather loudly. But Lady Rachel was not at all amused by her cousin and moved to stand at Esme's side.

"Lady Longton speaks very highly of your mother, Miss Colchester. I believe that, between them, they have been instrumental in raising a good deal of money at their most recent charity drive."

"Indeed, they have, My Lady," Esme said, grateful for the woman's concern but rather embarrassed and wishing that she could find some way to easily return to her sisters.

"I must say, I do like your gown, my dear," Henrietta Burton said in a shrill voice.

Esme turned to look at her and could see amusement riding high in her small and beady eyes. Esme knew immediately that it was not a true compliment and yet everything she knew of manners and etiquette demanded that she thank Henrietta Burton nonetheless.

No wonder Verity was so disenchanted with society and all its little demands. But Esme was a different person altogether, and she would behave in her own way.

"Thank you, Miss Burton," Esme said, hoping that the lighting was just dim enough that nobody would see her blushing.

"Really, it is so sweet. Had you not been here at a ball I would think you on your way to your wedding." Henrietta Burton spoke in a determinedly sweet and sickly tone, one disguised to thinly veil her spiteful intent.

So, the Marquis had discussed her before he had brought her into the little group and, if his friends thought they could be so rude to her, it was clear that he had not discussed her in glowing terms.

"It really is a very nice gown," Lady Rachel said hurriedly, but her gentle voice was drowned out by the laughter of the Marquis and Mr. Burton and his sisters.

"You must not take dear Henrietta seriously, Miss Colchester. She does have something of a bright sense of humor," the Marquis said but it did nothing to make Esme feel any better.

She felt small and stupid and wished for all the world that she could find some pretense for walking away from them. But she could think of nothing, so she simply nodded and smiled and wished that she could dissolve.

"Ah, I have been looking for you everywhere my dear," came a booming male voice at her side. "Do forgive me, one and all, but might I steal away Miss

Colchester for a few moments?" he asked, addressing the group.

"By all means," the Marquis said, although Esme thought he now looked a little disgruntled that another man had approached her.

The whole thing really was so very confusing; one moment he liked her, the next he did not.

But more confusing than that was the man at her elbow, holding out his arm to lead her away. Esme knew that she did not know him, they had never been introduced, and so she could hardly imagine what it was that he wanted with her.

"Please do excuse me," Esme said and bowed her head before taking the man's arm and allowing him to lead her away.

"Forgive me, Miss Colchester, for I know that we have not been introduced."

"No, we have not," she said waspishly, even though he had appeared as if to answer her silent prayer for some reason to escape. "But I have seen you before, have I not?"

"Yes, you caught me out at Lord and Lady Hollerton's garden party for staring at you," he said and laughed. "And you must forgive me, but I thought you were perhaps in need of a little assistance. I am not a man who would like to stand and see a young lady made a fool of for the sport of others."

"I am not at all grateful for that description of me, Sir," Esme said, her pride suddenly swooping down from above and wrapping its heavy wings around her.

"Forgive me, I did not mean to make matters worse," he said and looked at her apologetically.

He was a curious man and she wondered why on earth he had chosen to insert himself into her life. Ignoring the fact that he had, in a very practical sense, freed her from the situation she had been aching to escape, Esme chose instead to save all her annoyance for him.

She stared at him openly, defying every rule of etiquette she had carefully learned over the years as she made a very fine study of him. Esme realized that, had he not annoyed her so greatly, she might have found that face of his handsome.

He had fair hair and pale blue eyes, tanned looking skin, and a very firm jawline. He was older than the Marquis by some years, perhaps being a little more than thirty, and he was taller and broader than the Marquis, looking far less aristocratic because of it.

Esme had liked the Marquis' looks from top to toe. He was tall enough and slim with the slightly angular features of the aristocrat.

The man in front of her could have been anybody on earth. As handsome as he was, there was something in his manner which she assumed would make him a little rough, somewhat uncultured. And even though he had rescued her, he had done so in such a clumsy way that she thought his manners were very likely a little wanting.

"I do not understand why you thought it necessary to come to my aid," Esme said in a determinedly cool tone of voice.

"Forgive me, I did not know it was the current mode for young ladies to enjoy being treated so cruelly," he said and bowed, making ready to leave her.

"No, no," Esme said, panicking a little. "You cannot go yet."

"Why not?" he said, and she was certain he was laughing a little under his breath. "When I have displeased you so."

"You gave the Marquis to understand that we were acquainted. If you leave me standing here now, you will make more of a fool of me than ever."

"Then I am to rescue you from foolishness but be pleased to have you berate me for doing it?" Despite the harshness of his words, the man was smiling at her.

"Since you have caused all of this, I think it is incumbent upon you to see it through, Mr... Mr...?"

"Wentworth. George Wentworth," he said and bowed.

"Well, this is a fine introduction!" Esme said, knowing that her rancor was not entirely reserved for Mr. Wentworth.

Still, she was not yet ready to admit defeat as far as the Marquis of Longton was concerned. Forgetting Mr. Wentworth for a moment, Esme peered down at her gown and wondered, with the lace overlay, if it did not look little bridal after all.

Hardly able to believe that she had thought she looked so well as she had set off from her father's house that evening, Esme silently berated herself for her poor choice of attire.

"It is a very nice gown, Miss Colchester, and it suits you very well indeed," he said and looked at her with the sort of appreciation that made her blush.

"Not that it is any of your business," she said ungraciously.

"What you wear is none of my business, Miss Colchester. What I choose to see as pleasing, however, is." He was smiling at her again and Esme found herself growing more and more annoyed.

"I think I will return to my company now, Mr. Wentworth," Esme said simply, wishing she had never come out for the evening at all.

Everything had gone so dreadfully wrong and the fact was that she felt like crying.

"Would you like me to return you to the Marquis, or return you to your sisters?" he asked, and his tone of voice was less amused now and somewhat gentler and more concerned.

"I think I should like to be returned to my sisters," Esme said, knowing that she was admitting defeat but equally sure that there could be nothing to be gained from spending the evening in the company of Mr. Burton and his sisters.

She had decided by then the entire thing was their fault. Their spiteful influence had ruined everything.

CHAPTER 6

"*B*ut why did this Mr. Wentworth come to take you away?" Verity asked, not ready to receive anything other than the fullest explanation.

"He thought I needed rescuing." Esme shrugged dismissively.

"Is that because the Marquis and his party were laughing at you?" Verity seemed angry with Esme.

"Laughing at me? Oh, of course not." Esme was being defensive. "And I cannot work out why it is you seem angry with me, Verity," she added.

The Colchester women had all convened in Esme's

bedroom that night after the ball. All sitting on her bed in their nightgowns with their thick hair in long plaits, the women had gone over every part of the evening. Although it was true to say that Esme had left one or two things out.

"My dear, you did seem most uncomfortable. And those two young women were braying with laughter like donkeys, I could hear them from where I stood," Jane said gently. "Esme, you know you may tell us anything. We are sisters, are we not?"

Esme felt miserable as she watched the shadows from the two lit candles dancing on the walls of her chamber. Ordinarily, she found such a thing relaxing and comforting. But that night, the shadows looked taller to her somehow, darker and more ominous, as if even *they* found her ridiculous.

"I must admit, I was a little embarrassed in the Marquis' company. But not because of anything he did or said, really. It was the dreadful Burtons. His friend, Michael Burton and sisters, Eliza and Henrietta Burton. The sisters in particular were very rude, making unpleasing comments about my gown. They made me feel a little ashamed," Esme admitted and felt suddenly tearful although she blinked hard to avoid letting the tears fall.

"But that is disgraceful!" Jane said and reached across the bed to take her sister's hand. "You poor thing, how awful of them to behave in such a way. But what did the Marquis have to say about it all? Surely, he did not simply allow them to abuse you in such a way."

"No, no," Esme said, wondering at her determination to defend the man when he had not defended her. "His cousin, Lady Rachel Marlow, told me that it was a very nice gown. She is a very pleasant lady, I am sure. She reminds me greatly of the Marquis' mother."

"Then I am glad that she was there, my dear," Jane went on. "But perhaps it was for the Marquis to provide a comforting presence in that moment and not his cousin. After all, he was the one who invited you to join their party and so you were his responsibility."

Esme felt a little cornered; she was always a great student of etiquette and modern manners and now her own sister was using that against her.

The truth was, the Marquis really did ought to have taken more responsibility for her or, more to the point, perhaps never invited her to join his party in the first place. From the moment she had taken his arm and allowed him to lead her away, she really had become his responsibility.

"But never mind that now," Jane said, and Esme realized that her sister had sensed a little of her own upset and decided to talk about other things. "Tell us more about that handsome man who intervened."

"He did not intervene, Jane, he *interfered*. There was a very real difference, my dear," Esme said, and could feel herself becoming haughty at the very mention of the man.

So haughty, in fact, that it was as if he had suddenly appeared before her.

"I hardly even noticed him until he was leading you away. He must be a very stealthy sort of a man," Verity said with interest. "But surely he was close enough to know what was going on, otherwise he would have had no grounds to lead you away."

"He had no grounds to lead me away at all. Really, to behave in such a way towards a woman you have not even been introduced to." Esme knew she sounded disgruntled.

"I think it is rather exciting that he butted up against your ideas of etiquette just so that he could rescue you. It is rather romantic." Jane let out a girlish laugh.

"Oh, only you could see romance in such a rude man." Esme laughed, not entirely pleased to be talking about the man, but pleased not to be talking about her humiliation with the Marquis any longer.

"I suppose his actions might have been considered rude if you were having an entirely agreeable time with the Marquis and his party. But this man obviously saw your discomfort and sought to relieve it. Even if he was mistaken, surely his intentions were very fine." Jane was not ready to let go of the idea that this man, this perfect stranger, was somehow exciting.

"Yes, he was mistaken," Esme said, but quietly wondered if there was something to Jane's words.

"But it must have taken a good deal of courage for him to intervene or *interfere* as you call it," Verity added. "I do think you must give him that much credit at least, Esme. Unless you think that he only inserted himself into things to specifically upset you. Given that you do not know him, I can hardly think that *that* is the case."

"Although he is a stranger, I suppose it is true to say that he is not a perfect stranger," Esme said tentatively, knowing that Jane was about to seize upon her words hungrily. "For I have seen him before at Lord and Lady Hollerton's garden party. He stared at me."

"He stared at you?" Jane said, and even in the gloom of the pale candlelight, Esme could see her eyes widening with excitement.

"I did not notice at first, Mama did," Esme said, remembering how she had stared back at the man. "But then I did see him staring at me for myself. I thought no more about him until this evening."

"So, he already had an interest in you, my dear?" Jane said.

"I am afraid I do not find being stared at so very romantic, Jane."

"And yet you seem to find the idea of being mocked

for your attire much more so," Verity said solemnly. "Forgive me, sister, I am not coming down on the side of this Mr. Wentworth, or whoever he is. But I am still angered by the idea that the Marquis would lead you into a group of people who were so very rude."

"I do not think he can be blamed for what his company did. After all, he cannot have imagined that Eliza and Henrietta Burton would be so rude."

"Or perhaps you are just making excuses for him," Verity said, and Esme found herself resenting her youngest sister's propensity for common sense and speaking her mind.

"Really, it is nothing for the two of you to fall out about." Jane the middle sister, was always the voice of reason. "And to talk about this Mr. Wentworth once again, if you will allow me, I am bound to say that he was very handsome."

"Oh, Jane!" Esme started to laugh. "Then perhaps I should introduce the two of you."

"Oh no, I would not be happy to be introduced to a man, however handsome, when he is much more enamored of one of my sisters than I." Jane laughed mischievously. "But you must admit there is something about him." She peered intently at Esme.

"But you were nowhere near. If you had heard how Mr. Wentworth and I argued, you would not now think the whole thing as romantic as all that." Esme laughed.

"Well, I just think you should not dismiss him out of hand. I have high hopes for this Mr. Wentworth. I like the way he skirts around etiquette. And there is something a little mysterious about a man who behaves as he has done. I do not think you can rule him out."

"Rule him out?" Esme said incredulously. "Do you mean as a suitor?"

"Yes, of course," Jane said and clutched her chest dramatically causing Verity to laugh.

"But I know nothing about him. He could be *anybody*, Jane."

"He could indeed be anybody. And that is what I think makes him all the more exciting."

"Well, I am not excited by it."

"No, but that is only because you do not know where to place him on your list of suitable young men. You cannot put him into any category."

"Exactly that, Jane," Esme said, and wondered how it was that the two of them could see the same thing so very differently.

"Well, I for one hope to see Mr. Wentworth again. If nothing else, it would not hurt the Marquis of Longton to realize that you are greatly in demand."

"Oh, Jane, what a lovely thing to say." Esme leaned forward to put her arms around both of her sisters. "And how glad I am to have the two of you."

And for all her sisters' outspokenness, Esme really was grateful to have them both there.

CHAPTER 7

*L*ady Ariadne Stevenson, a baroness and a widow of the very merry variety, was always an exceptional hostess. She favored afternoon events and early evening events, this time hosting an evening buffet.

Her drawing room was immense and the seating extensive and comfortable. And Lady Ariadne always invited just the right number of guests, not so many that her drawing room was full, and not so few that the company was not good and varied.

Esme was in attendance with her mother and Jane, Verity having begged to stay home for the evening so that she might play a raucous few hands of cards with their brother, Amos. She claimed that she would much prefer it to the trouble of having to get herself ready to spend the evening with people she was not at all in the mood to converse with.

As always, their mother and father simply let her be. They really were the most tolerant of parents, although Esme wondered if that would necessarily be to Verity's advantage in the end. She was such a determinedly unusual character that Esme thought it perhaps not ought to be encouraged.

"Look, Lady Longton is here," Mrs. Colchester said, clearly pleased to see that fine woman in amongst the other guests. "Although you must remember, my dear, that even if I like Lady Longton very well, you need not accept any invitations that do not suit you."

Jane cast Esme a look as they both silently acknowledged the fact that none of them had spoken to their parents of the events of Lord Berkeley's summer ball. If they had, Mrs. Colchester would have been furious and might even have disallowed Esme the Marquis' company in future.

Neither Mr. nor Mrs. Colchester were so impressed

by titles that they would allow anyone in possession of one to be so rude to one of their much-beloved children. And knowing this, Esme was grateful that neither Jane nor Verity had gone to their parents with tales from the night.

"And look, her son is with her," Jane said in a flat tone as she narrowed her gaze.

Lady Longton had quickly spotted Mrs. Colchester and was hurrying over with a broad smile on her face.

"My dear Mrs. Colchester, how wonderful to see you again. I had no idea you would be here this evening. Really, what a treat!" Lady Longton was as effusive as ever and Esme thought it would be impossible for a person not to like that woman.

"Good evening, Lady Longton. How well you look," Esme's mother said genuinely. "Really, that shade of blue suits you perfectly."

Esme had always adored her mother and had always been in awe of the way she managed to give compliments so genuinely. And she only gave those compliments where they were due, not securing herself greater advantage by sycophancy. Nobody listening to Mrs. Elizabeth Colchester could think her anything but sincere.

As the two women continued to talk, Esme became aware that the Marquis was also making his way over. She felt her mouth go dry as she wondered how he was going to greet her this time.

"Miss Colchester, how nice to see you," he said, and Esme thought he seemed a little sheepish. "I wonder if I might have a few moments conversation with you?" he said, his eyes flicking momentarily to Jane who was standing sentinel and listening to every word.

"Yes, of course," Esme said, and moved a little away from her sister so that she and the Marquis might speak in private.

"I had really wanted to ask you to forgive me for the other evening, Miss Colchester. I was feeling greatly out of sorts, having been unwell for much of the day. I daresay that I was in very poor humor because I had really wanted to stay at Longton Hall that night. But that is no excuse, I should have intervened when Michael's sisters behaved so roughly."

"Yes, they *were* rather rough." Esme was surprised by

her own resistance to immediately accept his apology.

After all, this very apology was the thing she had dreamt of for the last few days, the thing she had hoped for more than anything. And yet there was something deep inside her that was thrashing around a little, a mutinous little part of her that wanted to spoil her plans to find and marry just the right sort of man.

"They can be a little envious of other young ladies, Miss Colchester, and had I been in better health I would have been quick to denounce their words."

"Well, I hope you are feeling a little better now, Lord Longton?" Esme said, willing herself to accept his apology and wondering why it was she could not do so directly.

"Indeed, I am feeling a good deal better." He smiled at her and Esme was lost again in just how handsome he was, not to mention the fact that his rueful expression made him look a little boyish. "And I hope that you will let me make amends by inviting you and your family to dinner at Longton Hall next week."

"Oh, how very kind, Lord Longton," Esme said, feeling herself flush with pleasure. "I know that we have no engagements so I can speak for my family, I am sure, in saying that we would be glad to accept any invitation you might make."

"I am so pleased, Miss Colchester. And I know that my cousin, Lady Rachel, will be very pleased also. She has expressed a desire to get to know you a little better and was sorry that she was not able to spend more time with you at Lord Berkeley's ball."

"I liked her very well indeed, My Lord," Esme said truthfully of the woman who had sought to relieve her distress. "And I would be very pleased to see her again."

"Then it is settled, Miss Colchester," the Marquis said with a broad and handsome smile. "I shall send the invitation to your parents tomorrow."

"Thank you." Esme felt her spirits soar.

Despite a few bumps in the road, Esme was certain that she was on the right path. And surely, any young woman looking to make a most sensible marriage must have the fortitude to survive any rough seas she might encounter on the way.

She was sure that she was over the worst of it now and that everything would be plain sailing from here onward.

But when she returned to her sister, Jane, she was a little upended to discover that the hopeless romantic seemed somewhat more cautious in receipt of the news.

"I suppose it is good that he has apologized," Jane said unconvincingly.

"He has not only apologized, sister, but he has invited our entire family to have dinner at Longton Hall. I think that is recompense enough, do you not?"

"For rudeness that should never have occurred in the first place?" Jane said levelly.

"Goodness, you are becoming more like Verity every day," Esme said waspishly for she could not understand why her sister was not happy for her.

"Forgive me, I do not mean to dampen your spirits," Jane said gently. "It really was very fine of the Marquis to apologize. Very gentlemanly."

"But?" Esme said, holding her sister's gaze firmly.

"But I cannot help but wonder about Mr. Wentworth." Her face eased into a romantic smile.

"I think you can safely forget all about Mr. Wentworth, Jane. I know I shall."

CHAPTER 8

"*A*re you all right, my dear? Shall I come with you?" Jane said with a look of concern.

"Oh no, I am perfectly all right, I would just like a little air. No, you and Verity carry on, I will be right outside the door, you need not worry," Esme said, wondering if her increasing nervousness at the idea of dinner at Longton Hall that evening was the root cause of her unsteady feeling.

She did not feel unwell, exactly, but rather like she needed a little space. The haberdashery where her sisters were pawing over cards of lace was a small shop which was so well-stocked that it appeared smaller still. But it was a little dark too, not having windows large enough to capture the glorious sunshine of the day.

"Would you not like a little lace for the gown you will be wearing to Longton Hall?" Jane went on, her own excitement at the prospect of such a fine evening growing day by day.

"No, the gown I have decided upon needs nothing further," Esme said confidently, although her mind immediately flew to her ivory gown with the lace overlay and she wondered if she had any idea about fashion at all. "But you take all the time you need, Jane. Really, I will be perfectly all right outside. It is just a little dark and a little stuffy in here for my liking."

"Very well, but just tap on the door or the little window if you need us," Jane said and kissed her sister's cheek before releasing her.

The moment she was outside, Esme felt a little better. It was a warm day, but the air was fresh and clean, and she took in great breaths to steady herself.

"Good morning, Miss Colchester," came a familiar voice.

Esme opened her eyes and was dismayed to see none other than Mr. Wentworth standing there before her.

"It is afternoon, Mr. Wentworth," Esme said in an irritated tone.

"So it is." He bowed and smiled brightly. "But perhaps I knew that already, my dear. Perhaps, as always, I sought only to annoy you." He laughed.

"Now why on earth would you seek to do that?"

"I would not," he said and smiled at her with curious warmth. "But I am certain that you would see it that way. I am very sure that I could do nothing that would please you, so perhaps I ought not to try."

"This is a most curious conversation, Mr. Wentworth," Esme said primly. "Perhaps I should remind you that we are barely acquainted. We were certainly not correctly introduced, Mr. Wentworth, and I think you perhaps ought to remember that. It is not quite the done thing for a gentleman to approach a young woman in such a fashion in the street when he is not entirely an acquaintance."

"So, because the introduction was not formally made by a third-party and with grand gestures and bowing and polite discourse, we essentially do not know one another at all?" He raised an eyebrow and laughed a little loudly for her liking. "What a curious society we are, my dear, when we are perfect strangers simply because the correct form of words was not adhered to on first meeting. What a shame it is that we will never know one another, however much time we might spend in one another's company. A great shame indeed."

"Mr. Wentworth, I am sure you think yourself very clever, but I do not."

"Goodness me, you are a very harsh sort of woman." He continued to laugh, and she wondered that he was not at all offended by her words. "I should not like to find out how it is you treat your enemies. Unless I *am* an enemy, of course."

"That is ridiculous. Of course, you are not my enemy, Mr. Wentworth. I do not know you well enough to be able to declare you as such."

"Perhaps now you think *yourself* a little clever, Miss Colchester?" His fair hair was thick and a little ruffled, as if he had ridden into town on horseback rather than in a carriage.

Esme surveyed him coolly, not at all embarrassed to look at him as she might have been any other man. But she was annoyed, and so embarrassment would very much have to take second place.

Esme could see that he was certainly a man of some means for his clothing was very finely made. It was simple, insofar as it was not ostentatious, but everything had been tailored perfectly and she found herself wondering exactly *who* Mr. George Wentworth was. And in the cold light of day, Esme had to admit that she found his height and broad shoulders rather more imposing than they had been when he had interfered in her business at Lord Berkeley's ball.

"Perhaps we *are* enemies, Mr. Wentworth," Esme said in a snap.

"Oh no, please do not take offense. I am teasing you, Miss Colchester." He bowed his apology.

"I do not think we are well enough acquainted for you to tease me, Mr. Wentworth."

"Not well enough acquainted? Not even when I have rescued you from an uncomfortable situation?"

"Rescued me?" Esme said in a voice that was rising with its incredulity. But perhaps she could ignore etiquette for the moment if this dreadful man intended to do the very same. "You rescued me from nothing. I did not need rescuing from anything at all."

"Except, perhaps, a little humiliation?" He looked less amused and more serious than he had done before. "But perhaps you think a good match is worth anything. He is a Marquis after all, is he not? The very *fine* Lord Longton."

Although his words felt a little mocking, his tone was anything but.

"If that is what you want in this life, Miss Colchester, then I wish you every success."

"I would thank you if I thought you meant it," she said and graciously.

"Perhaps it would be kinder of me to wish you every happiness instead of every success," he said and screwed his pale blue eyes up in thought. "For I rather think that your version of success will lead you to anything other than true happiness. But that is your mistake to make, not mine. I shall give up my interference, Miss Colchester." And with that he bowed deeply and turned to leave her.

With her mouth a little open, Esme watched him leave. There was something about his straight-backed bearing that was more confident than arrogant. But that would be as much compliment as she would ever give him, for he had angered her greatly.

And as she listened, Esme was certain that she could hear him chuckling to himself as he walked away, angering her further still.

Now why on earth would dear Jane see such a man as a romantic figure? No, the Marquis of Longton, the man who had invited Esme and her family to dinner, was a much better prospect.

CHAPTER 9

It was a great relief to Esme when dinner at Longton Hall not only began in a very welcoming and easy manner but continued in that vein throughout.

The Marquis had done everything in his power to make her parents, her brother, and her sisters, truly welcomed and at their ease from the very beginning. He had been bright and engaging, keen to talk hunting and riding with Amos and even a little estate management with her father.

And Lady Longton, entirely comforted by her son's fine behavior was kinder and sweeter than ever, relishing in her new acquaintances and clearly hoping that she might one day call them friends.

"Your estate might be smaller as you say, Mr. Colchester, but all the same matters must be attended to, must they not?" Daniel Winsford said as they sat around the enormous dinner table. "There are still staff to attend to, grounds and maintenance to be arranged, accounts to be done. In truth, I do not think your task any smaller than mine, Sir."

Esme was pleased that the Marquis had chosen to engage her father in such a way. It was a far cry from her first visit to Longton Hall and she was certainly pleased that her father had not seen the Marquis less than admirable behavior at Berkeley Hall. Although *she* had accepted his explanation on matters of health, she was certain that her father would not be quite so forgiving had he any idea of the little upset she had experienced along the way.

Esme caught an expression on Lady Longton's face and realized that it was one of contentment. Perhaps that fine woman truly thought Esme might one day be a suitable bride for her beloved son. Surely, *she* was a great factor in it all, keen to invite the Colchester family into their home and to maintain her burgeoning friendship with Esme's mother.

And so, Esme allowed herself a little daydreaming at the dinner table, looking around the immense dining hall and imagining herself there as the mistress of the house.

And as far as Lady Longton had explained it, this was the smallest of three dining halls in that fine mansion. Lady Longton had chosen it for its more intimate setting, leaving Esme wondering just how large the largest of the three dining halls might be.

This room was easily three times the size of their dining room back home and the furniture and decoration were immaculate.

The dining table was long and would easily seat twenty people, although their own settings had been spaciously arranged towards one end to maintain that intimacy Lady Longton had spoken of.

The ceilings were so high that their voices echoed a little. Although it was a little disconcerting at first, Esme had very quickly become accustomed to it. Surely, life in such a fine place as Longton Hall would require that she got used to such things. High ceilings, large rooms, and echoes were all part and parcel of moving up in the world.

After dinner, the party retired to the drawing room where little conversations broke out here there and everywhere. Mr. and Mrs. Colchester were handed glasses of brandy and shown about the large drawing room by the Marquis himself who pointed out various portraits and explained who each and every one of them were.

Jane and Verity were in discussion with Lady Longton, largely about the extensive grounds and some more in-depth points of botany. Esme smiled to herself, wondering how Verity had managed to turn their little conversation scientific. But Lady Longton, gracious as always, looked utterly enthralled with her younger sister and Esme began to feel truly at home.

This was what life was supposed to be when a young woman was embarking upon the road to marriage. That her family should get along with his was surely one of the more important aspects of the thing. And seeing how well they did get along gave her more and more confidence that her acquaintanceship with the Marquis of Longton was very soon going to become a courtship.

"I really was very pleased to hear that you were coming here tonight, Miss Colchester." Lady Rachel, who had remained sweetly quiet throughout dinner, took her arm and led her to the same couch she had sat on the first time she had been to Longton Hall.

"And I am very pleased to see you again, Lady Rachel," Esme said, feeling a little embarrassed.

After all, Lady Rachel had witnessed the humiliation at Lord Berkeley's ball and in remembering it, Esme could almost feel it once again.

"I had hoped to spend a little more time with you at the summer ball, my dear, but I understand entirely why you chose not to return to our little party." Lady Rachel looked a little ashamed which somehow stopped Esme's own sense of shame in its tracks. "I hope you do not think too badly of me."

"Of you, Lady Rachel? No, of course not. Why on earth should I?"

"For being in company with the dreadful Burton sisters for one thing." Lady Rachel winced. "To this day I do not understand why it is my cousin keeps company with Michael Burton and those appalling girls. They are extremely wealthy, one of the wealthiest families in England I would imagine, but their manners leave a lot to be desired. It is as if they think their great wealth allows them anything at all, even the right to be rude to others. They think themselves very clever and amusing, although I think they are anything but."

"I share your opinion of them, Lady Rachel, but I do not blame you for their behavior," Esme said and realized the time had come to show her gratitude for Lady Rachel's efforts on that night. "In fact, I must thank you for the way you tried to comfort me. It was not lost on me for a moment and I really was very grateful."

"I feel I should have been a little more forceful," Lady Rachel said, not ready to forgive herself.

"Not at all, you were perfectly comforting."

"I suppose it was not my place to be forceful on the matter, but rather my cousin's."

"Oh yes, he has explained himself and apologized," Esme said in a whisper, not wanting the Marquis to overhear her explaining his apology to anybody. After all, he would surely be offended by her giving away such a confidence. "And I understand entirely that he was feeling dreadfully unwell that night.

"Unwell?" Lady Rachel said with quiet disbelief. "Forgive me, Miss Colchester, but my cousin was in perfect health that night and every other since."

"Oh, I see," Esme said, feeling embarrassed again.

"Forgive me for speaking so plainly, Miss Colchester, but I would like to say that you should be somewhat cautious with my cousin." Lady Rachel's large brown eyes slid slowly across the room to settle on her cousin as if she wanted to be sure he could not hear her.

"Cautious?" Esme said, lowering her voice to a whisper also.

"I know he is my cousin and I ought to defend him robustly, but I know him well enough to know that he can be a capricious man, even a little cruel at times. He has been raised by his father to be a most entitled person. But his mother, who is my mother's sister, is such a sweet and warm human being that he has been touched by her influence also. Yet I am afraid that the result is that his moods swing quite markedly at times and it is not a pleasant thing for another person to have to endure." Lady Rachel's cheeks flushed a little. "You do seem like such a nice young woman, Miss Colchester, that I felt I should say something."

"Well, it is very kind of you to be so caring, Lady Rachel." Although Esme was hearing the very thing she did not wish to hear, she could not think ill of Lady Rachel for saying it.

There was an aspect of goodness about that woman which could not be denied and even if she were entirely mistaken about the whole thing, still, Esme knew that she had only spoken out of kindness.

Perhaps Lady Rachel did not know her cousin as well as she thought. After all, Esme hardly knew her own cousins well enough to claim their characters.

And there was a fair gap in the age too, with Lady Rachel being certainly in her middle thirties. With more than ten years between them, surely, they would never have been friends in childhood. Perhaps she truly was mistaken in her cousin's character.

Esme looked up when she perceived the Marquis and her parents approaching, ready to settle themselves down on the chairs and couches and join herself and Lady Rachel.

"I beg you would not say anything of this discussion to my cousin," Lady Rachel said in a hurried whisper. "I am not seeking to cause trouble, only to be sure that you have the full facts before making any decisions."

"Of course, Lady Rachel," Esme said and lightly patted her hand reassuringly. "And thank you kindly for your care." She finished before looking up to smile at the Marquis.

CHAPTER 10

*E*sme lay in her bed and stared at the ceiling. She had left the heavy velvet curtains in her chamber just a little open. It was enough that a thin slice of moonlight fell across the foot of her bed and the rustling leaves from the trees outside her window played out a pretty little shadow pattern on the ceiling above.

Her sisters had, quite naturally, spent a good hour in her chamber with her when they had returned from Longton Hall. They had both exclaimed what fine company the Marquis had been and had declared their admiration that he had shown so much respect and attention to their beloved father.

And even Jane said that the Marquis had become a

little more handsome because of it and Esme had smiled, thinking how easily Jane was tempted towards all that was good.

But she had said nothing of her conversation with Lady Rachel, at least nothing of all that mattered. In many ways, she wished she had found something about that good woman to dislike, for she was finding it very hard to reconcile her kindness with the words she had spoken.

Surely, she would not have said such things if they were not true. And had she not witnessed a little something of the Marquis' mood swings for herself? But Esme wondered if, should that be the extent of it, she might actually be able to cope well with a man such as Daniel Winsford.

Perhaps if it happened in future, she would not be so shocked by it. Perhaps she would learn to take it in her stride.

And then she was reminded of the words of the mysterious Mr. George Wentworth. His suggestion that she might well think any behavior acceptable if there was a good match to be had at the end of it.

In returning to the little scene outside the

haberdashery, the scene she had not mentioned at all to her sisters, Esme wondered if the Marquis and Mr. Wentworth were somehow acquainted. But the Marquis had given no sign at all that he knew Mr. Wentworth at Lord Berkeley's ball and so she could not imagine that they knew one another.

And yet, had not George Wentworth's words been a rougher version of Lady Rachel's? Did he know something of the Marquis which had led him to interfere at every opportunity?

How funny that she still thought of Mr. Wentworth as interfering rather than intervening. For in the end, what right did a perfect stranger have to intervene? And in such cases, was that intervention not interference after all?

Esme laughed to herself in the silvery darkness. What a thing to deliberate upon when there was so much else of importance to think about.

It had been such a strange night; one in which she had come leaps and bounds further towards her dream of the perfect union, and yet one of such disturbing revelations.

Esme thought of all her encounters with the Marquis

LOVE OR TITLE

of Longton and realized that they had been more pleasant than not. Even when they had first gone to afternoon tea and he had been reticent, he had cheered towards the end and made light conversation with her, even smiling. In truth, it was only the ugly scene at Lord Berkeley's summer ball which had given her any true cause for concern. And even then, she was sure that none of it was the Marquis' doing. As Lady Rachel had rightly pointed out, Michael Burton and his dreadful sisters were just that; *dreadful*.

But surely it was unwise on the part of the Marquis to keep company with such people, even if they were extraordinarily wealthy. What was money when there were no manners, no true class?

And even if they were wealthy, they did not hail from such a fine old home as the Marquis, and Michael Burton did not enjoy a title of any kind.

She could hardly see the point of the Marquis' continued friendship with such people, unless the fact was that he truly liked them.

Esme shuddered in the darkness, wondering what she should do. Being in Longton Hall had been like a fairy-tale to her, complete with a handsome prince and the promise of happiness for the rest of her life. And how welcome she would be with such a mother-in-law as Lady Longton! Even when the Marquis was in low spirits, surely, there would be comfort to be had in the company of such a fine and nurturing woman.

Once again, Esme was trying to talk herself into a life she was not entirely sure she wanted. But if she did not want it, what of all the years of careful study of the way of things? All her years of self-imposed strict adherence to the rules of society, the laws of etiquette? Were they to be wasted? Had she been so wrong?

And then she thought once again of George Wentworth. His seemingly rough manners, his interference without introduction. The way he offended her and laughed at her for her determination to live the very best life.

He seemed to represent the very opposite of everything she had worked towards. And yet she could not help but think about him, could not help but wonder who exactly he was and, better still, why it was he kept appearing in her life.

CHAPTER 11

George Wentworth did what he could to remain in the shadows, but he was finding it increasingly difficult given that the Earl of Melton's tree-shrouded lawns were lit by so many bright lanterns.

They hung everywhere, from trees, from statues, and there were even great torches staked into the grounds to shed light on the warm summer's evening.

It was something of an exciting departure from the normal run of events he attended. The Earl of Melton did enjoy a theatrical and quite often had his own family and friends put something together to lay on for the county. But this time he had gone a step further, employing the services of a traveling group of actors to put on a play outside.

The Earl's extensive staff had done a very good job of setting out enough seating and in such a way that they had turned the neat and enormous lawn into an outdoor theatre.

But George chose not to sit down when the time came, backing away a little from the crowd and watching the theatrical action whilst leaning heavily against one of the only trees which did not bear a lantern.

He had, of course, disappointed many people with his reluctance to be at the center of things. But that was the way when he was at home in Buckinghamshire; George was always the center of things, even in another man's house.

That was what was so appealing about Hertfordshire; if he crossed deep enough into it, the vast majority of people did not know who he was. His friends there knew well enough to introduce him quite simply as *Mr. George Wentworth.* And Hertfordshire was where his real friends were, those who did not seek to elevate their own status by introducing him so fully.

Buckinghamshire, on the other hand, was quite a different thing altogether. That was where everybody knew him by sight, everybody knew who he was. And everybody who invited him to an event did so to increase their own standing in the towns and villages of that fine county.

And at every event, George found himself doing everything in his power to politely avoid the attentions of young ladies whose only want in life was their idea of marital success.

George found his train of thought interrupted as the action on the makeshift alfresco stage had become more frenetic and just a little too loud. The actors were bounding this way and that, every movement they made exaggerated and every word they uttered seeming like a bellow to him.

Ordinarily, he knew that he would have enjoyed it. Even leaning against his tree and a little out of things, George would have allowed himself to be entirely immersed in the little performance, exclaiming with the rest, completely enthralled.

But he had found himself more irritated than usual that night to have been pursued by not one but three young ladies and their extraordinarily determined fathers. He knew all the fathers as acquaintances, of course, but each and every one of them had spoken to him in a confidential way, as a true friend might.

And each only to secure his own aims. Three fathers so keen to have their daughters raise their status in the world that they cared nothing for George's feelings on the matter. It was as if the whole world thought that nothing more than the appearance of suitability was of any consequence, and yet George was certain that it ought to be different. It *was* different, if that was what he chose it to be.

But as he leaned against the tree, not caring what the rough bark was doing to the back of his expensively tailored coat, George realized that he was in pursuit of the very sort of young lady he had always thought himself to despise.

For there was no denying that Miss Esme Colchester had very firm views on what made a man suitable in the marriage arena. It was the only explanation he could find for her determined defense of the young Marquis who had been so unforgivably rude to her.

She had seen a man who had not defended her honor or spared her humiliation and she had chosen to overlook it.

Was she not just the same as every other title hunting young lady he had ever encountered?

But he was certain that she was not. She had attracted him from the very first with her vibrant red hair and that air about her which declared a little confidence that the woman herself did not even know she possessed. It was as if her spirit was constantly being denied by her experience of the world around her.

The world around her demanded that she marry well; a man of wealth, title, importance. But perhaps her spirit did not see things that way. That little spark within her which held her head high even in the face of such adversity.

She had not crumbled at all when the Marquis' painful company had been so spiteful. She had not blushed or withered, and he had not heard her stutter. She simply stood demurely, her chin parallel to the ground, her green eyes giving nothing away of the feelings beneath.

But why had such a woman gone on to accept a further invitation from such a man? When she was clearly so much better than the Marquis, why did she persist in such self-defeating aims?

And that was why he could not simply dismiss her from his mind. That and the fact that she had shown him a little of herself outside the haberdashery in the little Hertfordshire town of Colington.

George smiled, the noise and action of the play now as nothing to him as he remembered the moment he had seen her standing there.

George had been on his way to see one of his oldest and dearest friends, Mrs. Constance Dalton, and could hardly believe his luck to stumble upon the red-headed beauty right there in the street.

And it was then that she had truly displayed the spirit within. As much as he knew he was right in all he said, he admired the way that she fought against him, dismissing him easily with her sharp-tongued intelligence.

George smiled, staring into one of the lanterns until it almost blinded him. It was easier to picture her that way. How cross she had been, and how she had raised her voice just a little the more he had annoyed her. And how energized George had been by such a fiery little exchange.

And in as much as he had walked away from her insisting that she must live her life if that was what she wanted, George Wentworth knew fine well that his days of interfering in the world of Miss Esme Colchester were far from over.

CHAPTER 12

With the summer in full swing, Esme found herself pleased that there were more than the usual number of balls that year in Hertfordshire. Ordinarily, during the London Season, things tended to go a little more quietly in the country. But this year they seemed set to enjoy as much merriment as the country's capital enjoyed. Not, of course, that Esme had ever attended the London Season. Her father had never been ambitious enough to push his daughters quite so far.

"Lady Asquith always puts on a very good ball, does she not?" the Marquis said to the little group gathered about him, Esme being one of them.

"Yes, but it is not quite London, is it?" Esme had

been dismayed to walk into Lady Asquith's small ballroom to discover that Michael Burton and his sisters were also in attendance.

Worse still, Daniel Winsford seemed very pleased to be in their company.

When they had first arrived, and the Marquis had ushered her into their little group, Esme had found herself somewhat dismayed not to find Lady Rachel there. If nothing else, she would have taken the edge off the disquiet she felt in Eliza and Henrietta Burton's company.

She had really wished for her sister's company at that time, but they were in conversation with their parents and Lady Longton. That good woman really did want the Colchester's to be a part of her world.

But Esme, although only a few feet away, felt as if she were in another county altogether. She blamed the Burtons entirely, for she was certain that it was their pernicious presence which made her feel so insecure.

"Well, it is not, is it?" Henrietta Burton continued, determined to have an answer. "Would you not rather be in London, Lord Longton? It is the place to be at this time of year after all, is it not?"

"I suppose I still enjoy the country in the summer, my dear Henrietta," he said and smiled indulgently at the young woman who wore more adornments than the average peacock.

She really was overdone with an expensive gown, a fulsome head-dress full of feathers, and a heavily jeweled necklace which was clearly worn to display her family's wealth.

But even so, Daniel Winsford seemed to like her. And it pained Esme to hear him talk to the woman and address her by her first name. She had no idea how many weeks or months of courting would have to be undertaken before he would address her as *Esme*.

Esme knew it was a petty jealousy, but she really did not like Henrietta Burton and she wished with all her heart that the man she had so much interest in did not like her either.

"I suppose it is all very well if you do not mind the fact that your company here will inevitably lack sophistication," Henrietta said and cast an all too obvious and lengthy glance in Esme's direction, her stare taking in every aspect of Esme's appearance.

But Esme was much surer of herself that evening, wearing a simple but striking dark blue gown with short sleeves and pristine long white gloves. She knew dark blue suited her rich chestnut hair and she was glad not to be wearing the ridiculous confection that Henrietta Burton sported on her head.

But nonetheless, she felt one or two other pairs of eyes on her and wondered how long her determination and confidence would hold out.

"But that is all part of its charm, my dear," the Marquis said and gave a braying sort of laughter.

Even though he had not specifically aimed his comments at Esme, still she felt the barb.

How could she not be a part of the unsophisticated company that Henrietta had alluded to and Daniel was laughing at? She was the only one in their company of her particular station in life. She came from a very fine family, she knew, but her father was upper-middle-class at best and she felt certain that Miss Burton was intent upon making the very most of the fact.

"Ah, the band is striking up," Henrietta said and deftly removed the small dance card from her velvet wristlet, tapping it gently and raising her eyebrows at the Marquis.

"I am ready to do my duty, Henrietta," the Marquis said humorously and bowed at her.

"As long as you do not forget your other duties." Eliza Burton tapped her dance card similarly and Esme realized that the first half of the Marquis' evening would be lavished upon those two appalling creatures.

Worse still, she was certain that each of the Burton women studied her for her reaction in the whole thing. And as determined as Esme was to remain dignified, she was certain that her countenance must have given away at least a little something of how she was feeling.

With her own dance card entirely empty, Esme simply stood as a spare on the edge of a group of people who seemed not to want her there. Michael Burton was loud and overbearing, and Eliza was watching her sister dance with the Marquis and continually commenting upon how fine they looked together.

The others in the party to whom she had been introduced seemed little interested in holding any sort of conversation with her either. She wanted to cross to her sisters but knew that Michael and Eliza Burton would surely be amused by it.

To take the edge off her own awkwardness, Esme looked vaguely about the ballroom. When she came eye to eye with none other than Mr. George Wentworth, she wondered if the evening could get any worse.

He smiled at her, but Esme did not return it. There were more than enough people mocking her that evening without her allowing George Wentworth to take his share.

It was at that moment that Esme realized she must make her excuses for a little while at least. Everything seemed too much to bear, and she knew that she should have listened a little more closely to Lady Rachel. This was undoubtedly one of those evenings when the Marquis' mood was going to swing in the other direction altogether.

And as much as she had tried to persuade herself that it would simply be a matter of getting used to it all, Esme knew that she was not quite ready to ride out such a storm. If practice was what it took, she knew it would be some time before she was proficient.

In the meantime, she would take a little air.

Politely excusing herself from her company without a word of explanation, Esme demurely made her way to the edge of the ballroom. She continued to stay close to the wall until she found herself at the immense double doors which lead out into the corridor beyond.

In no time at all, she found her way into the morning room and let herself out through the French windows and into the night.

It was late, and even though it was a summer's night, there was a chill in the air. She stood on the terrace and breathed deeply, taking in the rich and soothing bouquet of the night-scented stocks. Even though she could still hear the music and the chatter, it was distant, muffled, and the sounds of the night took over.

She heard an owl somewhere off deep in the woodland on the edge of Lady Asquith's estate. It hooted in a most determined fashion, waiting for a response that never came.

"It is a little chilly to stand out here, Miss Colchester."

Esme gasped in surprise and turned sharply to see George Wentworth standing a few feet away from her in the moonlight.

"For heaven's sake, are you following me?" she said in a snarl, realizing that she was aiming all her annoyance at one man.

"Yes, I am following you," he said plainly.

"Why?"

"Because you looked upset, Miss Colchester."

"I am not at all upset, Mr. Wentworth," she said, although she felt a little ridiculous saying it considering the tone of her voice.

Of course, she was upset, and of course she looked it.

"Forgive me, I have mistaken the whole thing," he said and took a step towards her.

"I am just taking a little air, Mr. Wentworth, that is all," she said in a less confrontational tone. "I only mean to be out here for a moment or two." She turned away from him and stared out across the moonlit lawn.

"Then at least take this for the time being," he said and, with her back still turned to him, she felt him lay his tailcoat over her shoulders.

The smooth skin of her shoulders was instantly warmed by the coat. Not for the protection it provided from the chill of the evening, but from the warmth of the man himself. The very warmth he had given to that coat as he wore it was the very warmth she now felt against her skin.

It was a most curious sensation, and one that was even a little pleasurable. For all the fractious nervous energy of the evening, she suddenly felt a little peace. It was the peace which came from quiet protection.

Esme bit her bottom lip and stared up at the moon; how Jane would have loved to hear her describe such an event and in such florid, romantic words.

"Thank you, Mr. Wentworth," she said, having no idea how to proceed with the conversation.

"I hope you will not lose many hours of sleep on account of the Marquis of Longton, Miss Colchester." It was clear that Mr. Wentworth was not at all lost for words.

"Oh?" she said, trying to keep her antagonism at bay whilst she enjoyed the warmth and protection that Mr. Wentworth's tailcoat seemed to symbolize.

"You are too fine a young woman for him, I am sure of it."

"Tell me, Mr. Wentworth, are you at all acquainted with Lord Longton?" She finally turned to face him, his shoulders looking all the broader as he stood in just his shirtsleeves and waistcoat.

"We have never been introduced, I am pleased to report," he said and chuckled.

There was something confident in his chuckle and she was not sure if it amused her or annoyed her. His eyes, which she knew to be pale blue, looked almost black by moonlight and she could see his fair hair lifting a little here and there in the light breeze of the evening.

"Then how can you state with certainty that I am too fine for him?"

"The evidence of my own eyes and ears does not need great swathes of time in which to come to a conclusion, Miss Colchester. And any other young lady might be pleased, even flattered, to be told that she is too good for a Marquis."

"Ah, but I do not know exactly who it is who gives this compliment, do I? If I did, it might make your compliment somewhat more believable."

"Do you really need to know my station in life to accept my kindness?" he asked, and she could hear the familiar amusement in his voice, the same amusement she had heard outside the haberdashery in Colington town. "Or do such things as kindness and caring not exist without a pedigree?"

"You are deflecting my question, Mr. Wentworth. And you are doing so by being very clever once again. You will remember, I am sure, that I am left a little annoyed by your deftly worded mockery."

"I do not wish to mock you, Miss Colchester. In truth, I only came out here this evening to be sure that you were all right. And now I see that you are, perhaps I ought to leave you."

"Who are you?" she asked again, determined to have some information about him at least.

"I am George Wentworth, Miss Colchester," he said and bowed.

And with that, Esme carefully removed his tailcoat and handed it to him.

"Thank you kindly for the coat, Mr. Wentworth," Esme said as she walked around him and back into the house.

CHAPTER 13

"This is an honor indeed, George," Constance Dalton said as she handed George a cup and saucer. "Two visits in as many weeks. Now either I have become more interesting in my old age, or you want something." The elderly woman smiled at him knowingly.

"You have seen through me, my dear Constance, and I will not insult you by attempting to bluff my way out of it." George laughed.

Constance Dalton was a distant cousin to his father, one he had always liked very much. And even when his father had passed away some eight years before, George had been determined to maintain contact with the fiery old lady.

She was a very fine woman and much admired and respected in Hertfordshire. She had always been one to speak her mind and it was clear that it was a trait which was only becoming more pronounced with age. But George liked that in a person, he liked to know exactly where he stood. And anybody in Constance Dalton's company could always be assured of that much at least.

"You are a good boy, George." Constance laughed gently. "So out with it, what are you looking for?"

"Information, of a sort," George began and, despite knowing Constance Dalton so well, he felt a little trepidation. "Information about a young lady, as it happens."

"Well, I never, George Wentworth has his eye on somebody, does he?" Constance Dalton said in a gently mocking tone.

"I am rather afraid I do, my dear," George said in an amusing way as if it were more an affliction than anything else.

"Well, who is the young lady? I presume I know her."

"You are as sharp as ever, my dear. Yes, I do believe you know her rather well. Her name is Esme Colchester."

"Oh, my dear Esme," Constance said enthusiastically. "Yes, I know the Colchesters very well indeed. And Esme and her mother regularly come to play bridge."

"I had thought as much," George said, his excitement rising. "But do they have a standing invitation, my dear?"

"Of course, they do," Constance said with some exasperation. "They have been coming to me for years. And Esme is a very fine bridge player, a very clever girl indeed."

"Which is why you like her, Constance," he admitted and realized that it felt quite wonderful to speak his feelings for the young woman aloud.

"And when are they next expected to attend? On what day do you play bridge, my dear?"

"On Thursdays, as a rule."

"And do Mrs. Colchester and her daughter attend every week?"

"Most weeks, but there are never any guarantees. That is the whole point of a standing invitation, is it not? A person may attend or not attend as their mood and circumstances suit."

"Yes, I suppose so."

"I take it you are looking for an invitation yourself, George?" she said, her shrewd eyes narrowed into slits.

"Indeed, I am, Constance. You really have seen right through me, have you not?"

"You are still a young man, my dear. It is easy for a woman of my years to see through the male of the species now with the benefit of experience and hindsight."

"You make us sound like very different beings, Constance."

"You are." Constance chuckled heartily. "But of course, you may have an invitation on any Thursday you wish. There, is it not time to improve your game? If you are to play bridge, I suggest you have a little practice."

"Indeed, it has been a number of years since I have

bothered with the game."

"But something tells me it is not the bridge that you intend to play, George."

"I would just like the opportunity to get to know Miss Colchester a little better."

"Then perhaps you ought to invite her to Buckinghamshire?" Constance said and gave him a knowing look.

"I am not quite ready to... to..."

"To admit who you are?" she supplied a little too helpfully.

"It is nice to be in a place where nobody really knows you."

"But I know you."

"Yes, and well enough not to give me away. I am fortunate to have many great friends here in Hertfordshire who allow me a certain anonymity so that I might enjoy society a little better."

"I am not so sure that you *enjoy* society, George. I think you are a spy, a watcher of society. You are a commentator, looking at the things which change and the things which always remain the same and I rather think you do so disapprovingly."

"Do you not think that there is much about the way we live which is ridiculous, Constance?"

"Oh yes, indeed I do." She laughed and paused to sip her tea. "So, you are going to get to know this young lady as *Mr. Wentworth* before you tell her anything about yourself. Do you not think that is a little unfair? After all, she is a very decent sort of a girl and one who I am sure would not be swayed."

"I believe that too, and yet still she is being wooed by a Marquis."

"*A Marquis?* There is only one I can think of in these parts," Constance said with an air of distaste.

"The Marquis of Longton."

"I thought as much." She shook her head. "But his mother is such a dear. And really, he was such a sweet little boy. But now that he has grown, he is too much like that father of his to be a good prospect for any woman. Can she not be given any little instruction upon his character?"

"Obviously, I have tried, but I am afraid that Miss

Colchester sees me as something of an adversary at the moment."

"But is your friend not staying at Longton Hall at the moment? Dear Peregrine's widow?"

"Yes, Rachel has been staying there for some weeks now and I know that she has tried her best."

"But Esme is still interested in the young man? Well, she is young and I daresay she sees some importance in making her way in the world. Is she really to be blamed for such a thing?"

"No, as long as she does not act upon it."

"And you think it is your business, George?"

"Probably not, but I have taken to the young lady. I see something better in her than this and I would like to stop her from heading into an unhappy world of her own making."

"Then let us hope, for your sake, that Esme sees things your way," Constance said and nodded urgently at the teapot, indicating that George should do the honors.

"Yes, I still have hope."

hen Esme was greeted warmly into Mrs. Dalton's drawing room, she was glad that she had decided to come after all. Her mother, usually her bridge partner, had declared herself to be too busy to come although she had no objection at all to Esme attending alone.

After all, it was a most sedate affair and Esme's parents knew exactly who would be in attendance. The same fine people who attended for a convivial afternoon of bridge each and every week.

Esme thought that the game would take her mind off things for a while. She had been secretly relieved that her beloved mother could not make it, for Elizabeth Colchester had tried to talk to her daughter more than once about her determination to set her sights on the Marquis of Longton.

Ever since Lady Asquith's summer ball, Esme was sure that her sisters had been petitioning their mother to intervene. Although they had not been a party to the little group on that night, they had both watched the Marquis intently and had, as was their custom, invaded her chamber that night with question upon question.

Verity had been particularly vehement, having no romance in her soul whatsoever. In truth, Esme was not even sure that it was blood which ran through the young Verity's veins and not pure common sense.

And as for Jane, she was almost tearful in the offense she had taken on her sister's behalf. How dare the Marquis dance the first two with those awful Burton girls, especially when they had already insulted Esme so thoroughly that the Marquis had been forced to apologize?

But Esme had brushed it all aside, admitting a little of what Lady Rachel told her previously. She had talked of Daniel Winsford's mood swings as if they were an affliction rather than a character flaw although it was clear that neither one of her sisters was convinced by her explanation.

And her mother had approached her more than once in the days which followed, gently reminding her that she was precious and beautiful, clever and interesting. The sort of young woman who ought only to marry a man who was truly worthy of her.

And as much as Esme thought she knew her own mind, she certainly had her own doubts. But she could hardly pick through it all with her sisters' determination to have her see things their way and her mother's loving care to make her wonder if she could ever make a right decision.

Not to mention the fact that she was hardly being courted by the Marquis at all. He drew her towards him at one moment and seemed to push her away the next. She wondered what his own thoughts on the subject were. Did he think them to be drawing closer?

"You have no partner today, my dear? Your mother is well, I hope?" Mrs. Dalton said, leading Esme by the arm to a table.

"She is very well, Mrs. Dalton. She is just rather

inundated with her charitable works at the moment and she sends her apologies that she is unable to attend today."

"Not at all, charitable works must be done," Mrs. Dalton said. "And I am sure we can find you a perfectly good partner."

"Will I do?" George Wentworth appeared quite suddenly and stood at the side of the empty chair beside her with clear hopes that he would be invited to sit down.

Esme was utterly amazed to see him there and, although she was sensible of the fact that her mouth was slightly agape, she seemed unable to control it.

"Ah, Mr. Wentworth. Are you acquainted with Miss Colchester?" Mrs. Dalton said in what seemed to be a rather unconvincing little piece of theatre.

"Yes, we are acquainted. Although it is true to say that we have never been properly introduced by a third party, Constance." His use of Mrs. Dalton's first name gave credence to Esme's suspicions that the two knew each other rather well.

"Oh, well then let me do the honors," Mrs. Dalton

said and laughed pleasantly. "Miss Esme Colchester, may I introduce you to an old family friend, Mr. George Wentworth."

"I am very pleased to make your acquaintance, Miss Colchester," he said and bowed so deeply that Esme almost laughed.

"How nice to meet you finally, Mr. Wentworth," Esme said and inclined her head before holding out her hand to indicate that he might sit. "Perhaps you would care to be my bridge partner for the afternoon."

"The very best of luck, my dear," Constance Dalton said, laughing as she walked away. "You are most certainly going to need it."

Not ten minutes into their game, Esme realized exactly what Mrs. Dalton had meant. George Wentworth was truly the worst bridge partner she had ever played with in her life and she knew that they would not last long before being thoroughly beaten.

"I realize I am not very good at this, Miss Colchester, but if you continue to roll your eyes so expansively, I fear they might roll clean out of your head and across the table," he said and smiled at her.

"Can you blame me, Mr. Wentworth? You have truly turned poor bridge playing into an art form." And despite herself, Esme laughed.

"Am I to take it that you would not be at all pleased to play a second game with me as your partner?" he asked and raised his eyebrows hopefully.

"In truth, I am not sure I have the required patience for such an endeavor."

"I must say, I rather like you when you are being a little sharp."

"You mean to say you do not like me the rest of the time, Mr. Wentworth?" For reasons she could not explain, Esme was finding herself enjoying their conversation.

It was certainly lively, if nothing else, and even a little fun. And she had to admit to being pleased to see him again, even if his initial appearance in Mrs. Dalton's drawing room had been somewhat disconcerting.

And for his part, Mr. Wentworth looked at his ease.

He was wearing black breeches and a fawn colored tailcoat and waistcoat which suited his tanned skin and fair hair very nicely. But even sitting down, his height could not be denied. Surely, a man who stood out as he did could not be as mysterious as he seemed to be?

She made a mental note to gently question Mrs. Dalton about the man if ever she had the opportunity. Perhaps that good woman would be able to provide her with one or two answers that would render him far less mysterious than he had been to date.

"On the contrary, I like you all the time, Miss Colchester."

"By which you mean that I am sharp all the time," she said and narrowed her gaze.

"You are a little too quick-witted for me, I fear." He laughed ruefully at having been caught out so easily.

When the game was over, Mr. Wentworth easily persuaded her to take a seat with him for a while and a little tea.

"So, I am bound to say that I believe you are

watching me, Mr. Wentworth. Until recently I had never seen you in my life and now you seem to be everywhere that I am," Esme said and realized that he truly was mysterious.

Was this excitement that she was feeling? But how could she be excited by somebody who was such an unknown quantity to her? He could be anybody. She truly knew nothing about him. And yet that little frisson of excitement persisted. She was beginning to realize that she had spent as much time in Mr. Wentworth's company as she had in the Marquis of Longton's.

"I watch everybody, Miss Colchester," he said cryptically.

"Why? To amuse yourself?"

"Partly," he said and leaned easily back in the armchair opposite her, his smile almost lazy and very appealing.

"Only partly?"

"I suppose I watch people partly to be sure of who I am dealing with. Social events are very much the same from county to county, all over England in fact.

I stand on the edge of it all and I watch the little pieces of drama being played out over and over again. The little dance that is danced to etiquette's tune. So yes, I am a little amused by it. But moreover, it gives me an idea of exactly who I am dealing with. I watch the little dances with interest, you see."

"You make very little sense to me at times, Mr. Wentworth," Esme said truthfully. "But perhaps that is because I still do not know who you are."

"I am Mr. Wentworth. George Wentworth," he said with a mischievous smile. "And tell me, how is Lord Longton?"

"I have not seen him since Lady Asquith's ball last week," Esme said, her spirit suddenly lowered by the very mention of his name. "I am afraid that I did not thank you properly for lending me your coat against the chill of the evening."

"You thanked me very well at the time, Miss Colchester, you need have no fear of that."

"Well, that is a relief if nothing else."

"You did not enjoy the evening," he said, and it was a statement, not a question.

"Not entirely." Esme was determined not to elaborate on it with the man who was still, in essence, a stranger to her.

"Tell me, have you spoken to Lady Rachel Marlow at all?"

"Lady Rachel?" Esme said, sitting bolt upright on the couch. "You know Lady Rachel?" She realized that her tone was a little accusing.

"Yes, I know Lady Rachel Marlow. She is the widow of a man who was my dearest friend, Peregrine Marlow."

"Forgive me, but I had not realized that Lady Rachel was a widow," Esme said and felt suddenly very sad that such a young woman had been made a widow.

"She does not speak of it much, Miss Colchester. They were greatly in love, you see, and she cannot trust her emotions to speak his name aloud in public."

"Oh dear, that really is terribly sad." Esme felt a little stab of emotion herself.

"Well, now that I have thoroughly saddened you, I

fear it is time for me to take my leave," he said and put his cup and saucer down.

"But why did you want to know if I have spoken to Lady Rachel?"

"I was just aware that she was staying Longton Hall, that is all," he said, and Esme was not entirely sure she believed him.

Did he know something of what Lady Rachel had told her when they had spoken so secretly at Longton Hall? And she could not escape the feeling that somehow Mrs. Dalton had more knowledge of the thing than she was admitting.

"I see," Esme said and nodded, realizing that she would get no further with him now. "Well, I am sure that you are determined to remain as mysterious as ever, Mr. Wentworth, so I will leave you to it." She returned to her old self once more. "And obviously I thank you dearly for your contribution to the bridge game this afternoon," she said in a tone which she hoped was amusingly sarcastic.

"It was a pleasure, Miss Colchester. My bridge services are at your disposal any time." He rose to his feet and bowed.

"I shall remember that." She laughed, inclining her head graciously to release him.

Some twenty minutes after he had left, and once Esme had finished her tea, she decided that it was time for her to leave also. Mrs. Dalton followed her out into the hallway to supervise the return of her cloak and chattered happily as she did so.

"I hope you have enjoyed the afternoon, Esme."

"Very much indeed, Mrs. Dalton," Esme said, wondering if now might be the time to ask one or two impertinent questions. "Forgive me, but are you very well acquainted with Mr. Wentworth?"

"I knew his father very well, my dear. They are a very fine family from Buckinghamshire. His father and I were distant cousins, which I suppose makes George Wentworth and I the same." She chuckled, and Esme knew by instinct that the dear old lady was being evasive.

"How lovely," Esme said and smiled brightly, knowing that she would get nothing further from Mrs. Dalton either and not wanting to risk offending a woman she thought of as a friend. "Well, it was certainly nice to be introduced to him properly at last," she said and held out her hands to take Mrs. Dalton's. "Thank you for another wonderful afternoon, Mrs. Dalton. Next week I do hope to have my mother with me."

"And thank you for coming, my dear. Your company has been a delight as always." Mrs. Dalton kissed her cheek before releasing her.

Esme walked the short distance from Mrs. Dalton's Colington townhouse to her father's carriage. The driver was staring wistfully into space, clearly enjoying the warm and sunny day.

He looked so content, in fact, that Esme thought it a shame to break the spell and interrupt him. She stood for a moment peering up at him, letting him have his last few moments.

"So, you asked Mrs. Dalton about me then, did you?" The voice behind her was so low and quiet that she thought for a moment she had imagined it.

But when Esme turned around, she found herself looking up into George Wentworth's handsome face.

"Yes, I did ask her," Esme said with some defiance.

"You spend your time watching people, Sir, whereas I prefer to take the direct approach."

"Indeed, you do," he said and laughed humorously. "But do you really need to know a person's background and public face before you can truly get to know them? You must ask yourself this, Miss Colchester; if that is how you choose to live, are you not missing out?" he said the last in a whisper, leaning in a little so that she felt his breath hot and warm against the side of her face.

Straightening up, he began to chuckle good-naturedly before bowing and turning to walk away.

She watched him leave with the same agape expression she had first greeted him with, in Mrs. Dalton's drawing room. He really was a mystery.

"Forgive me, Miss, I had not seen you there," the driver said, jumping down behind her and making her start. "Here you go," he said with a bright smile as he opened the door of the carriage and helped her inside.

CHAPTER 15

"Y ou are ready very quickly for the Marquis' ball, my dear," Elizabeth Colchester said when she found Esme sitting in the drawing room alone waiting for them all. "Do you not want to go?"

"Of course, we *must* go, Mama, we have accepted the invitation."

"That did not answer my question, Esme. If you do not want to go to the Marquis' ball, I will not make you. And I know I can speak for your father and say that he would feel the same."

"There is no harm in going to a ball, Mama. And I have heard from Lady Rachel that the dreadful

Burton sisters are not to be there. Michael Burton has some London engagement and they are to be trotting along behind him," Esme said with more than a hint of bitterness.

"I rather fear that the Burtons are going to become more and more of a problem as you get to know the Marquis and not less," Esme's mother said regretfully. "It is very clear to me that he would not be at all keen to give them up. And from what your sisters tell me, their poor behavior seems to have an effect on him."

"And yet you have seen him at his best, Mama. Is he not a fine young man of note then?"

"I cannot help but think that it is a simple matter of his being *of note*, my dear." Mrs. Colchester said and then held out her hands in front of her. "Do not look at me like that, my dear, for I am not trying to offend you or hurt your feelings. I just wish that I knew why it is you are so intent on the ideas that are held by society when neither your father nor I have ever sought to put such pressures upon you. There is nothing wrong in being proper, my dear, or even wanting the best for yourself and your children when they come along, but it must not be achievable only at the sacrifice of your own happiness. I am absolutely certain that life is not meant to be lived in that manner."

"Thank you, Mama," Esme said, and Mrs. Colchester looked surprised not to be on the receiving end of a volley of argument. "Your words are always the most sensible to me, always the worthiest."

"Well, for goodness sake, do not say as much to Verity. She sets a lot of store in common sense and she would not like to think that her silly mother held such a title." She laughed and reached out to lay a hand on her daughters' cheek. "You really are very beautiful, my dear, and I would never want to see you go to any less of a man than would deserve you."

Esme was suddenly taken by emotion, blinking furiously so that she would not cry and disarrange her appearance. But she could not help but rise to her feet and wrap her arms around her mother, holding her tightly, saying nothing in case her voice gave her away.

"Good girl, come on then," Mrs. Colchester said with

a smile. "If you are intent upon going to this ball, then I suppose we must move." She laughed.

When they arrived at the ball, it was to be greeted by an extremely effusive Marquis.

"Oh, my dear Miss Colchester, how very fine you look this evening," he said, smiling at her brightly as he surveyed what she thought to be a very plain outfit.

She wore a very simply cut gown of deep green with long white gloves and her hair was put up very neatly at the back.

"Thank you, Lord Longton," Esme said and smiled at him in the briefest way.

He looked as handsome and as immaculate as ever, but somehow it did not have the same effect on her. Esme found herself wondering if the mysterious George Wentworth might be somewhere in the great ballroom of Longton Hall. But of course, he had told her that they had never been introduced and he seemed so disapproving of the man that it was very unlikely he would accept any invitation that the Marquis might send out.

And for some reason, the idea that the man who had annoyed her so greatly in the past would not be there tonight made her feel a little low. She felt flat, as if the evening stretched out ahead of her interminably.

"As soon as I am finished greeting everybody, I will come and find you, my dear," he said, holding onto the hand she had held out to him just a little longer than she was comfortable with. "I have all sorts of people here tonight I would like to introduce you to."

"How very nice, Lord Longton," she said and inclined her head before following along behind her mother, father, and sisters.

Once again, her brother had taken the opportunity to make himself scarce and she began to think that dear Amos also knew a little something of the Marquis' character that he had seen fit to let her discover for herself.

"The Marquis seems to be in a very good mood this evening," Mrs. Colchester said when they were at a decent distance.

"I have only ever known him to be in a good mood," Esme's father said with a chuckle. "Perhaps it is my presence which suits him, my dear."

"Please, you must not," Esme said, wishing that she could enjoy her parents' gentle humor as normal.

But the truth was that she felt uncomfortable again, only this time it was not entirely because she felt out of place. She was not waiting for the Marquis' mood to swing in another direction, for she was certain that it would not that evening. What Esme was coming to realize was that she was not entirely sure she cared very much one way or the other.

True to his word, the Marquis appeared before half an hour was over.

"You must forgive me, it does take an awfully long time to greet people," he said as much to Esme's father as to Esme. "Mr. Colchester, I wonder if I might steal Esme away from you for a few moments to introduce her to some of my friends?"

"Of course," Edward Colchester said good-naturedly, clearly not a party to everything that her mother knew.

Esme was sure that if her father had known some of the worst of the Marquis' behavior, he would have dug his heels in about accepting any further invitations.

"Thank you," he said and bowed at Edward before holding out his arm for Esme to take.

Esme took his arm with a smile and allowed him to guide her through the ballroom, becoming almost dizzy with the number of introductions.

She seemed to be on his arm for the entire evening, being walked this way and that and introduced to more people than she could possibly ever remember in the future. And each time, he introduced her with pride.

"Please allow me to introduce you to Miss Esme Colchester, she is a dear friend of mine," he said more than once, keeping her arm in his almost perpetually.

He seemed bright and amusing all night, a perfect gentleman in every respect. He was attentive the entire time, always making sure that she did not want for something to drink or a little something to eat.

She was glad, in the end, when he had found it necessary to make his way out of the ballroom and answer some little problem that his footmen had encountered. He left her in the care of his cousin, Lady Rachel Marlow, and Esme was greatly relieved.

"You look exhausted, Miss Colchester," Lady Rachel said gently and took her hand. "Would you care to sit down for a few minutes?"

"Oh yes, please," Esme said, feeling her nerves to be shredded and her feet to be aching. "I have lost count of the number of people I have been introduced to this evening."

"Yes, I did see that Daniel was making you do the rounds, as it were." Lady Rachel laughed. "He seems to be in a very good mood this evening," she continued tentatively.

"Yes, he does," Esme said and realized that her tone entirely lacked enthusiasm. "Forgive my intrusion, Lady Rachel, but I believe we have an acquaintance in common." She changed the subject rather awkwardly.

"Oh yes?" Lady Rachel said, but Esme had an instinct that the fine woman already knew who she was talking about.

"Mr. George Wentworth," Esme plowed on regardless.

"Yes, George Wentworth is a friend of mine. Or at

least he was a friend of my husband," she said, and her voice took on a very quiet, wistful quality.

"I am terribly sorry, Lady Rachel," Esme said, remembering what Mr. Wentworth had said about Lady Rachel's continued deep love for her husband.

She would be very careful not to lead her into a discussion about him and have her upset so publicly.

"You are very kind, Miss Colchester," Lady Rachel said and nodded. "Yes, George Wentworth is a very nice man."

"I seem to bump into him everywhere, Lady Rachel."

"He is very fond of Hertfordshire of late, I believe. And he has a good many friends here, considering his own home is in Buckinghamshire."

Esme realized that there was nothing she could really ask about George Wentworth without it being plain that she was truly asking what his station in life was. She knew enough of his character to know that she liked him, after all. Any other questions would only be asked in order to satisfy her own need to know his status.

And where had that got her so far? Her

preoccupation with respectability, title, wealth, what had it brought her of worth? Nothing more than a handsome but entitled young man who was not in control of his own moods. Was that really a prize befitting the years of careful adherence to rules which had been decided upon long ago by people she had never met?

And so instead, she chose not to ask. She would simply let George Wentworth be himself. And if he ever chose to tell her more, Esme would be ready to hear him.

"I am bound to say, Lady Rachel, that Mr. Wentworth is quite the worst bridge player I have ever partnered with in my life," Esme said and was pleased when Lady Rachel laughed heartily.

"Oh dear, I can hardly believe he has displayed his appalling bridge skills publicly." Lady Rachel was highly amused. "And yes, he is a very poor player indeed. He has never taken the trouble to get to grips with the game, you see." Lady Rachel was still laughing. "He is far too busy making a study of everyone around him to concentrate on his cards."

"Yes, I can very well imagine that," Esme said and found her spirits lifting.

Perhaps it was Rachel's company, or perhaps it was the fact that she was talking about George Wentworth again. Perhaps it was even a mixture of the two. But this was certainly the first time she had enjoyed herself all evening and Esme realized that in itself was very telling.

"Forgive my intrusion into your business once again, Miss Colchester, but I would beg you to hear me out," Lady Rachel said, becoming suddenly serious and quiet again.

"Of course," Esme said and nodded enthusiastically. "You may say whatever you wish."

"Lady Longton is a very fine woman and I love her dearly. But she is so tender-hearted that all she wants in the world is to see her only son settled happily with a fine young woman who might go some way to easing his capriciousness and his little moods."

"She is very kind and clearly a very loving mother," Esme said gently.

"But as much as I love her, I would not see you sacrificed, not even to see that dear woman happy."

"I understand," Esme said, not wanting to put Lady Rachel through the embarrassment of having to explain herself fully.

"Daniel is a good man in his own way, but tonight he is seeking to please his mother. He loves her dearly, you see, and he remembers it more when he is not in the company of Michael Burton and his dreadful sisters. But just because he is behaving nicely this evening, please do not be taken in by it."

Lady Rachel looked down and even in the pale light of the ballroom, Esme could see her blushing.

"You must think me the worst kind of interfering woman. But really, I do like you so much and it would pain me to see you in a life that would not make you happy."

"I used to think that marriages had to be made in a certain fashion, Lady Rachel. And in all of it, if I am completely honest, such things as love and happiness did not really feature. I suppose I had the same list of quiet wants and demands that any other ambitious young woman might have. Nothing out of the common way, perhaps a little ambitious for my station, in truth."

"It is all very understandable," Lady Rachel said graciously.

"The thing is, I am not as sure as I used to be that I have the thing right. It is a funny thing, but I have two sisters, as you know. Jane is a hopeless romantic and Verity is the most unromantic common-sense filled young woman you might ever wish to meet. I had always thought myself to be somewhere between the two, but in actual fact I realize I have been quite different. I have been somewhat gullible, I suppose," Esme said, feeling a little shaken inside to hear the truth of herself spoken aloud from her own lips. "I believed it all, you see. The very moment I was out in society, I took every single part of it on board and held it close. Everybody talked of finding just the right sort of young man to marry. I very quickly fell in line with it all and learned everything I could about how to behave and what to say. How to appeal to a man of consequence, I daresay."

"You do not need to try to appeal to anybody, my dear. You are a very fine young woman in your own right."

"It is very kind of you to say so, Lady Rachel. I just wish that I had allowed myself to enjoy the privilege of coming from a family where no awkward expectations have been placed upon me. My parents truly want nothing more than for me to be happy, and I know from my experience in society that it is a rarity to be treasured. But I have not treasured it. I have simply continued along the path as if I am under the greatest pressure to succeed. And now I believe it has led me here, right to Longton Hall. And in coming here, I have raised the hopes of a very dear lady and it pains me to think of it."

"You must not think of it too much. After all, Lady Longton is perfectly well aware of her son's flaws and I think, in the end, she would have been greatly surprised to find herself with a daughter-in-law like you."

"I do wish this evening could be over. Seeing the Marquis as he is now, so pleasant and excited, I feel the most tremendous sense of guilt. The truth is, I have never particularly regarded him highly. Not Daniel Winsford, the man. I never really bothered to get to know him at all."

"And he has never bothered to get to know you either, otherwise he would not behave as he does."

"When it is all finished, Lady Rachel, I do hope that you and I can remain friends," Esme said and truly meant it. "I have been very touched by your kindness."

"Have no doubt of it, my dear. We shall remain friends."

CHAPTER 16

George Wentworth had hovered on the edge of the Colchester estate for more than an hour. He had crept onto the grounds earlier and slid a note addressed to Esme beneath the front door. He could only hope that it had reached her hands although he was certain, given everything that Rachel had told him about the Colchester family, that her parents were not of the type who unscrupulously read their daughters' letters.

Still, if they did, it would certainly take some explaining. And as the time passed, he began to worry that he had done something that would see the woman he had come to care about so greatly in trouble.

Until, that was, he saw her and one of her sisters walking arm in arm in the direction of the little woodland where he had remained out of sight. Surely, they could only be making their way in response to his desperate little note requesting that Esme meet him secretly. He had expected, of course, that she might bring one or both sisters. As much as he was sure that she was changing, that spirit of hers rising up to the fore, he still knew her to be a little too cautious to be found alone with him.

Well, he would take what he could get.

"Miss Colchester?" he said, coming upon the sisters the very minute they entered the woodland. "You received my note?"

"I am here, am I not?" Esme said and looked at him with cool amusement. "What is so urgent, Mr. Wentworth, that you linger here on a cool autumn day without a cloak?"

Esme looked very beautiful. She wore a simple fawn colored gown with long sleeves, a matching velvet Spencer jacket, and a bonnet of a little darker color. The autumn shades suited her pale skin and red hair beautifully and her green eyes looked like jewels peering out at him from beneath the brim of her bonnet.

"I suppose I have come to interfere in your life once again, Miss Colchester," he said, spreading his hands out wide and looking at her earnestly.

In response, Esme looked at her sister, Jane, who nodded imperceptibly before walking ahead a little to give them a few moments alone.

"I suppose I ought not to be surprised, Mr. Wentworth. Interfering in my life seems to be chief among your hobbies of late."

"Do you mind very much?" he asked. Holding her gaze, he was impressed that she did not look away.

There it was again, that spirit. That little defiance that rested inside her, barely beneath the surface, always ready to break out and show itself.

"Not as much as I used to," she said and gave him the briefest of smiles. "But I suppose that could all change at any moment, largely depending on what it is you have to say this time."

"As sharp as ever, Miss Colchester."

"Well, at least I can be sure that you still like me as long as I am being sharp."

"Quite so," he said and realized that he suddenly felt nervous.

This was no longer the casual interference of days gone by. This was something so much larger, a true interference in the course of her life.

"Well?" she said and tilted her head to one side expectantly.

"I have come to advise you not to accept the Marquis of Longton's proposal of marriage," he said in a rush of words.

"What proposal of marriage, Sir? As far as I am aware, he has made none."

"But I think he might."

"And what on earth makes you think that, Mr. Wentworth?"

"As I said before, I make a study of people."

"And you have studied the Marquis of Longton so closely that you believe him on the point of proposing?" She looked at him incredulously.

"As much as you would seek to laugh at me, Miss Colchester, I can see the truth of it in those green eyes of yours. You have seen his capriciousness and you know how easily he is excited. You know him to be capable of a sudden proposal, one made without a particular courtship of any kind."

"*Capriciousness?*" Esme said and leaned her head back to look up at the sky through the myriad of branches which were now losing their leaves to autumn. "What a funny word to use."

"I do not think it a particularly funny word, Miss Colchester," he said and felt a little confused, even wary if he was honest.

"It is funny, but that is just how Lady Rachel Marlow described him just two nights ago. I was a guest at Longton Hall, you see, for the Marquis held a ball there. I was fortunate enough to have a few minutes with dear Lady Rachel and she described her cousin in just such terms as you have described him."

"You suspect me of something?"

"It is not a suspicion, it is certain knowledge. You,

Lady Rachel, and dear Mrs. Dalton, have a connection that I do not quite understand. And as part of that connection, I am perfectly well aware that you have all discussed me at length."

"But you must understand that both Lady Rachel and Mrs. Dalton care for you greatly. It is not idle gossip," he said in defense of his two finest friends.

"And you need not defend them against me, Sir, for I know well that they are very fine women. But they have information that I do not; an understanding of you that I have not been allowed."

"What do you mean?"

"They, at least, know who you are."

"Ah, here we are again. You seek once again to identify my status. Well, I am not a Marquis," he said with a little flash of annoyance that he would rather not have given away.

"And you misunderstand me if you think that I am only interested in that much information about you. That is far from what I meant, Sir," Esme said, her bright eyes flashing with annoyance. "If it needs explanation, then you may have one," she went on, holding a hand out in front of her to steady his tongue when he was about to interrupt with his apology. "My meaning is that they know you. They know your past, your life, the trials and tribulations, the joys, the sorrows, everything. I am not so fortunate as to have such prized information. As much as you have sought to interfere in my life, however openly and honestly you have done so, you have managed to do it without giving me a single shred of who you are."

"But I..."

"Yes, you have said, I know enough about you already. You are undoubtedly a kind man and a good man, if only evidenced by your association with two of the finest ladies I have ever met. You are also amusing, annoying, clever, witty, intelligent, and one of the most irritating men I have ever met," she went on mercilessly. "So please understand that I *do* have the capacity to glean that much about a fellow human being."

She was becoming furious.

"And I personally do not care whether you are the king of England or a farmer's son. I like you well enough, Mr. Wentworth, I am simply becoming hurt that you do not trust me with the details of your life and furious that you would seek to interfere in mine when you clearly do not believe in me." And with that, she turned on her heel and began to march sharply away.

"Please, Miss Colchester..." he called out after her.

"Jane!" She turned, only to call out when it was clear that she had forgotten she had left her sister adrift in the woods.

Jane hurried along, crossing George's path and shrugging at him as she went. But her eyes were bright, and her smile was wide. No doubt Jane Colchester had heard every word and had seen what he had felt; that there really was something special between George and Esme.

He only hoped that she would calm down for long enough to see it.

But for now, the decision very much lay in Esme Colchester's lap. Rachel was certain that the

Marquis would be proposing any day and all George could do was stand back now, his final piece of interference done, and hope that Esme Colchester would make the right decision.

And George was as certain as he possibly could be that his own happiness depended on it entirely.

CHAPTER 17

"But it was romantic, Esme!" Jane said the following morning.

"I cannot believe we are still discussing this," Esme said with a roll of her eyes, despite the fact that she was actually enjoying it all.

When Jane had chased her back into the house after her brief meeting with Mr. Wentworth, both women were excited. Even though she had argued with him, Esme had felt the romantic flames that Jane had confidently declared to be present.

"I just hope he does not take your tongue-lashing to heart. Perhaps even now he is vowing never to set eyes on you again," Verity added in such a level tone that Esme and Jane laughed heartily.

"Oh, but what if he does?" Esme said. "I would wish I had never said it all except that I meant it. Oh, Jane, do you think he is gone forever?"

"No, of course not." Jane was firm.

"There you are!" Their mother said, bursting unceremoniously into Esme's room where all three sisters had been since breakfast. "Esme, you have a visitor. Did you not hear him approaching?"

"Oh, he is here!" Esme said excitedly. "But look at me! I must change. I cannot go down to him like this!"

"Come, I will help you," Jane was already on her feet and opening the door to the tall wardrobe.

"There is no time, my dear. The Marquis seems awfully agitated," Mrs. Colchester said hurriedly. "I think you must come now."

"The Marquis?" Esme said with a horrified look.

"Who were you expecting?"

"I... I... well..." Esme looked desperately at Jane.

She had forgotten all about the Marquis of Longton. Her head had been so full of George Wentworth and her excitement at what she was so sure were blossoming feelings on both sides, that she had not thought of the Marquis once.

"I think you must see him, Esme. He might not be the most pleasant man at times, but he deserves to hear your answer face-to-face." Her mother spoke knowingly and gently.

"My answer?" Esme was beginning to panic.

"You must realize this is why he has come. Just be honest with him, Esme." Mrs. Colchester took her daughter's arm and gently led her away.

By the time she reached the closed door to the drawing room, Esme felt decidedly unwell. She felt hot and flustered and heartily wished that she had never made her mind up to impress the Marquis of Longton at all.

"Do you want me to come in with you?" her mother asked gently.

"No, you are right. I must tell him the truth and I think it will be easier if we are alone. I do not want to

157

humiliate him in front of others, even if he has chosen to do just that to me on more than one occasion," Esme said, finding a little justification in her words which gave her a modicum more strength.

She gently pushed the door open and went inside, closing it behind her.

"Ah, Miss Colchester," the Marquis said and smiled, although it was clear to Esme that he was certainly feeling nervous.

"Lord Longton," Esme said and smiled briefly.

"You must be able to guess at my reason for being here today. I mean, I have never come to your father's estate before." He laughed, and it seemed his nervousness was growing.

"I do know why you are here, Lord Longton, and I must beg you not to ask the question you have come here to ask me."

"But I have come here to ask you to marry me, Miss Colchester," he said, and his sudden smile was a little too garish to be handsome.

"I realize that, My Lord. But I would beg you do not ask me, for I cannot agree to it."

"You need not be concerned, I will speak to your father and I am certain that he will allow it." He laughed and shrugged. "What father would not allow their daughter to marry a Marquis?" He looked around their drawing room, tiny in comparison to his own at Longton Hall, and Esme detected the vaguest hint of superiority.

If nothing else, it would give her the determination to do what must be done. It might not be Longton Hall, but her father's home was a good one and Esme decided there and then that she would never set her sights on a man purely because of his title and status again. This was her mistake, and it was hers to rectify.

"My father would agree to anything I ask as long as it made me happy, Lord Longton," Esme said in a firm but gentle tone. "But I am afraid that I do not believe that you and I would be happy together."

"And why is that?" His tone changed so suddenly to one of annoyance that Esme was taken aback.

"Because of this, Lord Longton. Your moods are so changeable, and I could not spend my life one minute being admired and the next despised. It is not good enough that you continually apologize for your behavior towards me, for I cannot continually forgive it."

"You take things too seriously, my dear. If it irks you so much, I can change it," he said, and Esme realized that he was slowly but surely attempting to bully her into it.

"Either way, I would not be happy. I do not love you, Lord Longton, and I know that I never shall," she said, knowing there was nothing for it but the absolute truth. "It is no good marrying for anything other than love. You have a very fine home, Sir, and a title to be proud of. But what I am looking for in my life is something very different."

"Then you are a fool, Miss Colchester. Nobody will make such a fine offer to you again, you can be sure of that."

"I know that you are angry, and I am sorry for it, but I never made you any promises. We were not courting, Sir, although I have been very pleased to be invited to your home and spend time with you and your kind mother. And even if we had got along better than we do, so soon a proposal was surely something that you could never have expected to be accepted."

"I am a Marquis, I could ask a perfect stranger to marry me and she would," he said with overblown pride.

"Then I wish you the best of luck, Lord Longton."

"I do not wish you the same, and I promise you that I will make you a pariah wherever you go. You and your family will not enjoy such invitations as you have received in the last years, believe me." And so, his mood swung again, showing the Marquis of Longton for the man he truly was.

"You must do as you must, Lord Longton. I do not appreciate such threats, but I cannot stop you from making them, nor can I stop you carrying them out. That is a matter for you and your conscience," she said and turned to leave the room.

As she reached out for the door handle, the Marquis seized her wrist roughly. Esme tried to shake herself free and turned to look into his eyes.

"If you do not take your hands off me now, I shall shout for help. And then, when you are out of this house, your behavior will become known and I will make *you* a pariah," Esme said and glared at him, her stare utterly unflinching.

"You will die an old maid, and you will deserve it," he said petulantly as he released her, pulled open the door himself, and marched promptly out of the house.

CHAPTER 18

"*E*sme, Esme," Verity said, bursting into her room the following morning with a curiously excited look on her face. "You must hurry up and get dressed."

"Verity, that is what I am trying to do. Goodness, what has got into you?" Esme turned to give an amused look to her maid, Violet. "Go down and eat your breakfast and I will join you shortly."

"There is no time for breakfast, Esme," Verity said, holding out a sealed letter in front of her. "This was on the doormat when I went downstairs. It must be from him."

Esme took the letter from her sister and peered at her

name written in beautiful copperplate script on the front. She had seen that handwriting before, she knew it so well that she did not need to take out his last letter from its hiding place and compare the two. It was George Wentworth, she knew it.

"Well, open it," Verity said urgently, surprising her sister with this most un-customary display of excitement.

Esme opened the letter, allowing Violet, who knew almost as much about the Colchester women's lives as they did, to remain present. She was a kind young woman who had been in their service for many years and she had always kept the girls' confidences.

"What does he say?" Verity asked in a hiss as Violet moved a little closer to her mistress.

"He is out in the woodland again and he wants me to meet him," Esme said and could not keep her smile to herself.

"Well, it is my turn to come with you, Jane has already had her share," Verity said firmly. "Come, you are dressed now, we will sneak out before breakfast."

"You seem a little excited, my dear," Esme said teasingly.

"I just want to see how this is all going to end," Verity said and shrugged.

"Will I do, Violet?" Esme asked and looked herself up and down.

"You will do very well, Miss," Violet said and gave her a warm smile of encouragement.

* * *

IN NO TIME AT ALL, Esme and Verity had put on their cloaks and bonnets and darted across their father's estate.

"Just think of it! Jane will be jumping up and down with annoyance. She is still asleep and I am out here getting all the news!"

"Verity, you really are naughty sometimes." Esme laughed. "But I am glad you are here with me."

"I wonder how long he has waited?" Verity asked in a whisper.

"Yes, perhaps he has been more than an hour," Esme shuddered. "And it is awfully cold."

"So, I should wait here? Out of the way?" Verity asked, coming to a standstill as soon as they were in the woodland.

"Yes, please. He is only there, you see?"

And sure enough, George Wentworth, wearing a heavy coat to guard against the cold of the autumn day, stood leaning against a tree. As soon as he saw her, he straightened up and bowed.

"Good morning, Mr. Wentworth. I must say, you are awfully early today," Esme said, unable to stop herself from teasing him.

"Well, I could not sleep, Miss Colchester." He looked so handsome with his ruffled fair hair and his pale blue eyes.

His mighty frame was no longer intimidating to her, rather it was something of a comfort and an attraction.

"Tell me, have you ridden all the way here from Buckinghamshire?"

"Ah, you know where I come from then?"

"It is all that Lady Rachel and Mrs. Dalton would give away. That you are a fine man and you come from Buckinghamshire." Esme smiled and could see that the harsh words of their previous exchange had been forgotten.

"And if I invited you and your family to have afternoon tea with me in Buckinghamshire, would you come?" He took another step towards her until they were just inches apart.

"Yes, of course, I would." Her voice sounded a little hoarse.

"Even though you do not really know me? Even though you do not know my station in life?"

"But I *do* know you, Mr. Wentworth. I know everything that is important. Not the things I used to think were so, but the things which truly *are*. And I know that I have never enjoyed company and conversation such as yours in my life. It does not matter to me where you live or how you live."

"Then expect my invitation in the post, Miss

Colchester," he said and suddenly took her gloved hand in his and raised it to his mouth to kiss it.

Despite the encumbrance of the glove, Esme felt a wave of excitement ripple through her from head to toe.

THE FOLLOWING MORNING, all three Colchester sisters were up early, dressed and awaiting the first post of the day. Amos, also up early but for very different reasons, looked at them askance when they walked into the dining room for an early breakfast.

"I am going hunting, dears, what is your excuse?" he said with a hearty chuckle as his sisters took their seats at the table.

"Nothing," Esme said a little too quickly.

"Oh, so you are not waiting for the post then?" he asked, peering around his sisters to look out of the window. "Well, I suppose I shall make my way out and intercept it instead."

"No!" Esme said and jumped to her feet, much to her brother's amusement.

She dashed out of the dining room, through the little entrance hall, and out through the front door. By the time she reached the post carriage, she was breathless and red-faced. The driver looked down at her from his seat with confusion before jumping down and handing her the Colchester family post.

"Thank you so much," Esme said with a bright smile, confusing the poor man further still before she turned and ran back for the house.

She ran all the way through the house until she was back in the dining room, flinging herself down into one of the chairs as she sorted through the handful of letters.

When she saw the beautiful copperplate script that she recognized so well, she dropped the remaining letters down on the table and hurriedly opened it.

"Forgive me, but is that not addressed to our mother and father?" Amos was on his feet and leaning over her shoulder.

"Yes, but it is meant for me," Esme said, knowing that neither one of her parents would mind at all.

"Very well," Amos said, still leaning over her to get

the first glimpse at what was so exciting. "Although if it comes to it, I shall deny all knowledge of this moment."

"Well? Is it the invitation?" Jane asked, gripping her teacup so hard it was a wonder the handle did not come clean of.

"It is," Esme said, and her heart began to pound; she could hardly believe what she was reading.

"Read it out!" Verity said with exasperation.

"Mr. and Mrs. Colchester,

I would like to invite you and your family to Gorton Hall in Buckinghamshire on Wednesday of this week for afternoon tea. I should be very glad for your attendance and look forward to meeting you all.

Yours sincerely,

George Wentworth, The Duke of Gorton."

Jane shrieked with excitement and Verity sat back in her chair with her mouth open wide. Esme looked up at her sisters, suddenly mute.

"I cannot keep up," Amos said humorously. "One minute you have a Marquis proposing to you and the next you are invited to tea by a Duke. Goodness, you really have made a study of society, my dear." He laughed and kissed the top of her head. "But I am glad you turned down the Marquis. You really are too good for him. Time will tell if the Duke of Gorton is good enough."

"Oh, he is good enough. He was always good enough," Esme said under her breath.

CHAPTER 19

"My goodness, but you have led us to some very fine homes lately," Edward Colchester said with a laugh when he climbed down from their carriage in front of Gorton Hall. "Even the Marquis would be impressed with this."

"I hardly know what to say," Esme said as she stared up at more than a hundred windows like sightless eyes peering down at her.

She felt tiny standing there beneath so large a building, a little intimidated, and somewhat breathless. But she could understand now why it was that George Wentworth spent so much time in anonymity. What young woman would not *give* anything, *say* anything, to be mistress of such a place? Had she herself not been just such a woman before her experiences of life had taught her what was truly important?

A neat and very friendly looking butler appeared at the top of the stairs, smiling politely as he greeted them and showed them into the largest entrance hall that Esme had ever seen.

She was pleased that the Duke did not put on a ridiculous display of footman in fine livery and all the other pomp and ceremony that the Marquis of Longton had thought so necessary. And he was not waiting inside the drawing room but hovering outside as if it was important to him to somehow meet them halfway.

"Mr. Colchester." The Duke bowed. "Please, do come in." He ushered the family in and nodded to the butler who promptly left them. "I am sure that tea will be with us in no time."

"You have a very fine home, Your Grace." Edward Colchester bowed in response. "And it is a pleasure to meet you."

"It is a pleasure to meet you, Sir. And Mrs.

Colchester. Welcome to Gorton Hall. I am very pleased to finally make your acquaintance."

"And I am pleased to meet you, Your Grace." Mrs. Colchester was the same as she ever was.

She smiled warmly, was perfectly poised, and clearly at her ease.

After greeting her brother and sisters in the same vein, the Duke turned to Esme.

"I hope you are well, Miss Colchester," he said with a smile, his pale blue eyes warm and amused. "It is a great pleasure to see you again and I am very pleased that you and your family have accepted my invitation."

"And I am pleased to see you again, *Your Grace*," she said and raised her eyebrows.

"Perhaps *Mr. Wentworth?*" he said and winced.

"Oh no, not at all," Esme said in a teasing tone. "It is most definitely *Your Grace*."

The afternoon tea seemed to fly by, the conversation never once running dry, and much merriment and amusement was enjoyed by all in the Duke's retelling of his curious courtship of Esme Colchester.

After the invitation had been received, of course, Esme had been forced to admit everything which had passed between them to her mother. Mrs. Colchester claimed to have known that there was somebody in Esme's heart all along, somebody who was most certainly not the Marquis of Longton.

With the afternoon tea finished and nobody seeming to want the day to come to an end, the Duke asked the family if they would care for a tour of his home. He assured them that it was a pleasure his housekeeper never rejected, claiming that she had been there longer than he had and likely knew more about it.

And so, the family followed an extraordinarily pleased housekeeper as she masterfully led them around all the wonderful sights to be seen at Gorton Hall.

"And there are some wonderful portraits in this room, Mr. and Mrs. Colchester," the housekeeper said brightly. "It is just a shame that this room is little used, and they are hardly ever seen. But perhaps His

Grace might consider bringing them out now and again, swapping them for some of the others."

"As you see, I am a very simple man," George whispered to Esme as the two of them kept to the back of the group. "Simple enough that I am bullied daily by my housekeeper. I will, of course, rotate my portraits from now on."

"How very humble of you, Your Grace," Esme said in a whisper.

As the family followed the housekeeper into the side room to look at rarely-seen portraits, George gently took Esme's arm and held her back. She turned to look at him and smiled.

"Thank you, Esme," he said in a whisper. "Thank you for not knowing who I was and liking me anyway."

"I suppose I am not the woman you thought I was. Although I cannot blame you for thinking it, for I was certain I *was* that woman myself."

"No, that was the reason I could not stop interfering. I do not know why, but I was certain that you were very different. And it looks as if I was right, does it not?"

"Yes, it does," she said.

Without another word, he reached out to lay a large hand on her cheek and he kissed her just once on the lips. It was so fast that Esme wondered if it had happened at all. And yet despite the brevity, she could still feel the warmth his lips had left behind on her own and knew that she would enjoy many more such kisses in the years to come.

"So, what are we celebrating this time?" Edward Colchester said when the family and friends had taken their seats around the dining table at Gorton Hall. "There always seems to be something to celebrate."

"Well, they are already married, Papa, so it cannot be that," Jane said, and Esme was certain that her most romantic sister had already perceived the reason for the family being called there on that day.

"It most certainly is a celebration, Mr. Colchester, and I am glad that you are all here on this day." George rose to his feet and lifted his glass in preparation of a toast.

"Goodness, this is exciting," Mrs. Colchester said, and if she realized the reason for the celebration too but was doing her very best to hide it.

Esme knew that she had never been happier in her life. Married to George for more than a year now, she had never once regretted her decision to spend the rest of her life with him. He did not change at all, not even when he was finally declared to her as the Duke of Gorton. He was still just *Mr. Wentworth*, her beloved George. He was funny, he was clever, he was the most dreadful teaser.

"Oh, George, you really are dragging this all out," Lady Rachel Marlow said with humorous exasperation. "You like to play your part so well you really ought to be on the stage." At which everybody began to laugh.

"Oh, give him his moment, Rachel." Mrs. Dalton, so integral a part in bringing the two lovers together, was also a much-treasured guest.

Esme looked around the table at her wonderful parents, her fine brother and beautiful sisters, and her dear friends, Rachel and Constance, and felt truly blessed. She would never have imagined that finding herself with the title of Duchess would be the very least of all she had to be grateful for. She had even wondered if there was still anything left in the world to experience. And yet it seemed that happiness was drawn to her now like a moth to a flame.

"All right, all right, I will get on with it," George said to yet more amusement from around the table. "I had something of a speech prepared, but in truth it was a little long-winded and rambling, so I am just going to say the thing plainly."

"George," Esme said with a sigh. "I wish you would."

"Very well," he said, his time for teasing over. "I am so very pleased that you can all be here today with my wonderful, *beautiful* wife and I to celebrate the news that we are expecting our first child."

Esme felt tears spring to her eyes when the entire table erupted into effusive congratulations and surprise, despite the fact that they must surely have all realized long before George's announcement.

But it was just like all of them to throw themselves into Esme's happiness and she only hoped, as she looked at her wonderful sisters, the women she missed so much day-to-day, that she would be able to return that wonderful favor one day.

Now that she had everything in the world she wanted, all she could ask for was that her sisters would one day enjoy that same happiness.

"Congratulations, my darling," George said, leaning towards his wife as he took his seat again. "I do love you, Esme," he whispered into her ear as the excited chatter reached its crescendo all around them.

"And I do love you, Mr. Wentworth. I love you with all my heart."

"I promise you that I will always make you happy."

"I am sure it is a promise that will be easy to keep." Esme smiled at her husband, her heart swelling with so much happiness she thought it might burst.

If you enjoyed this book you will love A Race Against the Duke

THE LADY and the Secret Duke Preview

. . .

THIS NOVEL LENGTH book is FREE on Kindle Unlimited or just 0.99 for a limited time only. Grab your copy now. **The Lady and the Secret Duke**

* * *

"I THINK I can quite understand your mother's reservations about it all, Rebecca," Oliver Brentwood spoke with a little caution.

"Oliver, I cannot think that three small children in the parlor for a few hours a day is a problem. If learning to read is off-putting to any potential suitor my sister might find..." Rebecca Beaumont felt a little rankled by the notion. "Then she would be better off without him."

Of course, it was her mother, rather than Oliver, who had put her in a bad mood. Isadora Beaumont had been skirting around the subject for weeks and now, finally, she had turned to her husband to lay down the law. And, as always, she had tried to make it sound as if she had done her best for Rebecca, but that her father had been adamant. Only, Rebecca knew better than that.

"What did your mother say?" Oliver was trying to sympathize but missing the mark somewhat.

"She said that my sister has ambitions and that it was only fair they be realized." Rebecca could hear her own dismissive tone. "Really, Diana is not at all ambitious. And even if she had such notions, I would never do anything to upset her plans."

"I know how dear your sister is to you." Oliver smiled.

"I mean, *really*, it is not as if Diana would be entertaining potential suitors in the parlor, is it?" Rebecca blew out a great puff of air in what she immediately realized was not a particularly ladylike fashion.

"I think it is just the idea of it all. I do not think for a moment that your mother imagines that the son of a baron, or whomever it is who finally comes calling upon your sister, will stumble upon the three ragged little children you teach. I think she is likely just concerned that news of it might reach them, that is all. But then, I suppose it is hardly a secret that you run a little dame school, is it?"

"No, it is not a secret. But I do not see why it ought to be. When did it become a crime to harbor a wish to help those less fortunate?"

"It is not a crime, my dear, not even in the best of society. But charity is more acceptable in its fundraising form for young ladies, rather than in its practical form. Could you not turn your hand to something of that nature instead? After all, you would still be helping people." Oliver shrugged, and Rebecca could not help but feel a little patronized; she always did when he called her *my dear*.

Whilst Rebecca knew that fundraising was an important part of charity work, it was not that which gave her the greatest satisfaction. She had been educated very well and was grateful for it. She always wanted to find ways to share that education with people who had not been quite so fortunate.

Nothing had given her greater pleasure than to teach the three young pupils who arrived at her family home, Wisteria Manor, three mornings every week. They were poor children, although not as desperately poor as others in the largely rural community. More than that, they were so eager for the gift of reading that they listened with such rapt attention every day. Rebecca felt sure that she had not paid such attention at that age, when she had been receiving a very much fuller education than they were.

They were an inspiration to her and she could not bear the idea that there would be no place for them to continue their learning.

"I would not be helping in the same way. There are more than enough young ladies who busy themselves with gathering the funds, but how many of them do anything to really help? And who is going to teach Violet, Robert, and David now that my mother has successfully closed the door in their faces?" Rebecca could not hide her anger and anguish.

"I am afraid that there is nothing that I can do about it, Rebecca," Oliver said, looking somewhat pained to be the person on the receiving end of her annoyance.

"Forgive me, Oliver." She turned to look at him and smiled apologetically. "I suppose it is all very raw at the moment and I am still angry with my mother."

Rebecca cast her eyes down the long lawn to where her mother and sister were clipping late spring blooms, much to the consternation of their gardener.

"You are forgiven, Rebecca." Oliver cast a quick look down the garden also before hurriedly taking Rebecca's hand in his own for a moment and squeezing it.

Rebecca knew that she ought not to take things out on Oliver. After all, he had always appeared to be most supportive in everything that she wanted to do. He had been courting her for almost a year and never once had he openly objected to her ideas regarding the education of poor children.

Oliver was a handsome young man, tall and slim with pale blond hair and beautiful green eyes. He had a keen, intelligent face, which had appealed to her greatly when they first met. He was from a family as wealthy as her own. The two of them looked set to have a happy and comfortable future together and Rebecca felt sure it was only a matter of time before the two of them became engaged formally.

"And I cannot think that Papa has any real objection

to the three children coming to Wisteria Manor. He has always seemed so very keen to hear the details of the lessons and to find out how they are getting along. I can only imagine that my mother has talked on and on about the thing, determined to have her way until finally he has given in. Even Diana did not seem to have any particular objection. In fact, she seemed quite surprised when I told her that Mama had got her way and my dame school was finished."

"Yes, but Diana cares a great deal for you, however different the two of you are," Oliver said brightly, and she knew it to be true. "At least the two of you have not fallen to arguing about the thing, at any rate. Diana is simply following your mother's instructions in the art of finding the most suitable husband imaginable."

"That is what Diana wants more than anything, and I would not begrudge her it, really I would not. She has such a kind and sweet nature and I feel sure that she felt a little dismayed at the plight of the three children."

"I do not see how they are suffering any more than they had been before you had begun to teach them, Rebecca. After all, having the ability to read would not have been anything that either they or their parents would have expected out of life, is it?"

"But do you not see the unfairness of that? Do you not see how cruel it is that a person, simply by dint of their circumstances at birth, is denied that most basic pleasure? The world is closed to a person who cannot read, Oliver, because they do not even have the faintest chance of improving themselves."

"But that is the way of things, Rebecca. That is how society works and I think there is very little that you can do about it. I admire your heart, truly, but I do not think that you can change a system that has been in place for hundreds and hundreds of years. Probably has always been in place, if we are honest about it."

"I am sure that I cannot change everything, Oliver, but perhaps I can change a little. Perhaps I can look about me and change what I see. It is not much, granted, but if there were more people willing to do it, things would change. That is what change is all about."

"And what am I to do whilst you are changing all that you can see about you?" Oliver asked, and

Rebecca saw a look on his face she had not seen before.

"I would not neglect you, Oliver. Surely you must know that."

"But I would never be first, would I?" He seemed genuine in his argument, so much so that Rebecca felt a little sense of disquiet.

"Of course, you would." She smiled at him broadly, fully expecting that he would return her smile.

When he did not, Rebecca began to wonder what he really thought of all that she wanted to do in the world. "We would be side-by-side, Oliver."

"Side-by-side in what?" Oliver still looked serious.

"I am determined not to give up, despite my mother's best efforts at making me do just that." Rebecca smiled excitedly, determined to tell him of the plan which had been growing ever larger in her mind since her little schoolroom in the parlor had ceased to exist.

"I do not see how you can go against her, especially not when your father has now taken her part."

"I do not mean to return to the parlor with just three little pupils. I should like to try for something a little bigger, something that will benefit very many more of the poorer children in the outlying villages."

"How so? What do you intend to do?"

"I thought I might try to secure a building. Not to purchase it, you understand, but to find an old building that is unused and offer to pay rent on it."

"For what purpose?" Oliver seemed a little suspicious and Rebecca hardly knew whether she ought to continue.

"Oliver, I have lately read a piece published by a man called Samuel Wilderspin. It is called *On the Importance of Educating the Infant Poor*, and it is a most inspirational read."

"Who is Samuel Wilderspin?"

"He is an English educator and he believes that children ought to learn through a variety of experiences, even including play, to develop their intelligence and refine their feelings. He is trained in infant education and has lately begun a little school in Spitalfields in London with his wife, Ann. It is a school that is run for the poor children of the area and it is entirely free."

"So, it is a *Ragged* School, so to speak?"

"No, it is very different from the system of ragged schools," she continued tentatively. "It provides a somewhat more formal education, introducing subjects beyond reading. It would include arithmetic and some simple mathematics and other subjects of interest. Perhaps even some history. From what I have read, it is a most thorough system."

"And you intend to emulate that here?" Oliver did nothing to hide his incredulity.

At that moment, Rebecca felt crestfallen. With only his tone, it seemed to her that Oliver was clearly telling her that he did not believe for a minute that she could manage such a thing.

She had truly hoped that he would have been more interested in what she had to say, in fact, she had almost been convinced that he would be. After all, he had been kind and sympathetic when she had told him of the loss of her little dame school and she had assumed that he would be pleased for her to have alighted upon an idea even better with which to replace it.

"Yes, I think it is something certainly worth aspiring to." Rebecca felt unsure of herself, as if she ought not to tell him any more about it.

Of course, when she had first read Wilderspin's publication and found out a little more about the school he had set up himself, she had been inspired by the fact that he had worked alongside his wife to ensure its smooth running. From that moment, Rebecca had been convinced that Oliver would be only too pleased to help her, to support her in a very much more practical way from now on.

Perhaps she had allowed too many little fantasies of a happy husband and wife building up a small, free school of which they could be inordinately proud. She had assumed that Oliver Brentwood would think such an endeavor extraordinary and worthwhile. It had never occurred to her that she would find herself wondering whether she ought to even mention it to him. She wanted to ask, but she did not want to hear his answer if it was to be no.

"That is quite an aspiration, my dear. After all, did

you not say that this Samuel Wilder, or whatever is name is?" He looked at her for confirmation.

"Wilderspin," she said simply.

"Did you not say that this Samuel Wilderspin is trained in infant education? You are educated, certainly, but are you sure that you are educated to such a degree?"

"I am content that I have wit and intelligence enough, Oliver. It is not a simple thing to teach a person to read and yet I have managed it more than once. I agree that teaching is an art, but it is one that I think I could master very well. And as for my knowledge, I was fortunate enough to be very well educated. My father saw to it and I am very grateful." Rebecca felt a little as if she were defending herself and she did not like the position.

Oliver's countenance seemed to have darkened a little and she wondered if he really was as pleased to be courting an intelligent young lady as he had always claimed to be. Perhaps he had simply tolerated the idea of the dame school because, to him, it might well have seemed a little hobbyist. Nothing more than a dilettante flailing about for a short-lived purpose, a fleeting interest that would soon be discarded.

"And would you not find it difficult to teach a larger group of children? After all, you have managed no more than three so far, have you not?"

"I have only taught three because that was all there was room for in the parlor here at Wisteria Manor. Had I the room for more, I would most certainly have taken them."

"You have a good heart, Rebecca, and I am sure that you would have taken in as many children as you could fit. But that is not my question. My question is could you *manage* to teach more than three? It is not a question of space, my dear, but rather one of maintaining the interest of so many children. In small quantities, I am sure that they behave very well indeed but have you considered how difficult it might be to contain a class of very many more children, especially poor children."

"What difference does it make if they are poor?" Rebecca was beginning to wish that she had not begun the conversation.

It seemed clear to her that Oliver was going to find

an objection to each and every part of it. Once each objection had been dealt with, he moved easily to his next. As their conversation ground on, Rebecca began to lose her confidence a little. What if she really could not manage to teach a large group? What if Oliver was right? And since it seemed now that he would not be as interested in assisting her in the whole thing as she had hoped he would, would she really be able to manage it alone? Could she try to enlist the help of other like-minded ladies?

"It is simply that they have very different manners, Rebecca. I think they are likely rougher and a good deal much more difficult to control. I was talking to Louisa Staffordshire about this very thing just last week and she would agree."

Rebecca felt her anger flare but she reined it in and answered as logically as she could. "I have not yet found that to be the case, Oliver. Quite the opposite, in fact, because they are somewhat more grateful for the education that they had not seen as their right." Rebecca could hear a little bitterness in her tone. "Still, something to think about on another day, is it not?" She concluded as cheerfully as she could, not keen to end such a wonderful afternoon on the terrace of Wisteria Manor on a sour note.

"Indeed, it is," he said a little more brightly. "However, if you continued in your quest, a sensible man might find himself drawn to another young lady altogether, a young lady like Louisa Staffordshire."

Rebecca could not believe what he had just said. Could not believe the hurt that stabbed into her chest and her face fell as tears almost came to her eyes. Her mouth was opening and closing and she saw the look on his face. It was chagrin but something more there was a touch of manipulation.

"I think perhaps that we should change the subject," she said.

"It is all inconsequential now," he said. "I doubt very much if you will be able to continue with your school. Let us think of ways to raise funds for these poor needy children."

Rebecca could not believe that he seemed pleased with himself. As if he had done her a favor and she was pleased when the visit ended shortly after. Suddenly, her future was changed. How could she continue to see Oliver when he felt so differently to her? How could she let him go when he was the man she knew she would marry? How would she cope if her dream was taken away?

GRAB THIS NOVEL length book for FREE on Kindle Unlimited or just 0.99 for a limited time only. **The Lady and the Secret Duke**

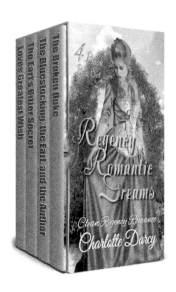

Love at Morley Mills 6 Book Box Set including an exclusive book in one 6 book collection FREE on Kindle Unlimited.

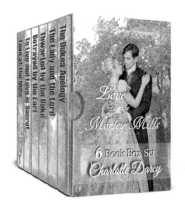

Love Against the Odds an 11 Book Regency Box Set

ABOUT THE AUTHOR

I hope you enjoyed these books by Charlotte Darcy.

Charlotte is a hopeless romantic. She loves historical romance and the Regency era the most. She has been a writer for many years and can think of nothing better than seeing how her characters can find their happy ever after.

She lives in Derbyshire, England and when not writing you will find her walking the British countryside with her dog Poppy or visiting stately homes, such as Chatsworth House which is local to her.

You can contact Charlotte at CharlotteDarcy@cd2.com or via facebook at @CharlotteDarcyAuthor

Or join my exclusive newsletter for a free book and updates on new releases here.

Printed in Great Britain
by Amazon